Jane Ellen's Path

~ by ~

Sue McDougald Watson

PublishAmerica
Baltimore

ISBN: 1-4241-7112-1
PUBLISHED BY PUBLISHAMERICA, LLLP
www.publishamerica.com
Baltimore

Printed in the United States of America

Sharon, I know all this is foreign to you, but I hope you can enjoy the story.

Sue McWatson

Chapter I

When Jane Ellen reached the door, Mama wasn't there to greet her. Tugging the hand-me-down suitcase into the front room, Jane Ellen saw her grandmother huddled up to the fireplace, totally oblivious to the fact that anybody had entered.

Jane Ellen spoke her name, causing Mama to jerk around and gasp. Oh, God, this looked bad! When Jane Ellen reached the chair by the hearth, the normally cold, unresponsive Mama sprang to her feet, grabbed the tall, stately student who wore the homemade dress and designer coat, hugged her close, and burst into tears.

"Lord God, chile, I didn't know you was on the place. I been settin' here studyin' what's gonna happen, and I never heard the car."

"What's wrong, Mama?" a dismayed Jane Ellen managed to ask her grandmother, reluctantly pulling back from the embrace.

"It's Mr. George, baby. He done lost everything," a weary Mama sighed as she collapsed back into the chair. "Cattle prices been off the last few years, the drought two years in a row, and no hay for winter feed done brought him down. The bank foreclosed yesterday. Him and Miss Pat moved out the big house; they gonna stay with Miss Pat's mama and papa. Mr.George tryin' to find work in town, and Miss Pat eb'n tryin' to hire on at the courthouse or the lunchroom at school."

Jane Ellen was certain all this was a bad dream. It couldn't possibly be real. She hadn't heard from Lynn in three weeks, but she chalked it up to finals and preparations for graduation in the spring. Poor Lynn. Jane Ellen had to go to her.

"Mama, where's Lynn?" a confused Jane Ellen asked. "I need to see her."

"She with her folks at her granny's in Selma. She ain't took the news so good. Too, Mr. Zell Green been after her to get married. Since she don't know how she gonna make her way now, seem she gonna do it. There ain't no money for her last session at college, Mr. George say, and Mr. Till agreed to send her if she marry Zell soon as she graduate."

Jane Ellen felt physically ill. This last part had to be a nightmare! Lynn had written earlier in the year about Zell's marriage proposal, but she assured Jane Ellen she couldn't tolerate the boorish racist and wouldn't be caught dead going out with him, much less marrying him. She had been dating a finance major, and while he wasn't wealthy, he was bright, a scholarship student from Mississippi, and Lynn had sounded quite taken with him—even going so far as to promise to introduce the two of them when he came home with Lynn Christmas. So much for those plans!

Jane Ellen had always loved Christmas vacations at home with her family—both her birth family and her adopted white family in the big house, especially Lynn. This time, however, the holidays did not bring the traditional gift box with fancy smelling paper, and not once did she see any of the Wambles family. She did venture up to the house on her third day home, but padlocks on all the doors prevented her going inside. She couldn't even go onto the back porch. She did sit in the swing under the old oak tree in the back yard and cry as she hadn't done in years.

While she was in the swing worrying about Lynn, Mr. George, and Miss Pat, it occurred to her for the first time that

Mama was now without a job. She had not considered that fact. Springing to her feet, she ran all the way home.

Bursting through the back door, she once again took her grandmother by surprise. "Mama, I'm so sorry! I haven't once thought about your job. I was just thinking about the Wambleses. What will you do?"

"Chile, don't worry 'bout me," Mama reassured her. "Come February I'll be sixty-two. I'm gonna draw my Social Security check. I got a little saved up, and with what me and your Uncle Jack grows in the garden, the milk and butter from Jack's cow, I'll be all right. It might be kinda nice to sleep past 4:30 some mornings. I might could get use to that. I'm gonna be all right. It's them pore white folks I'm worried 'bout. They ain't never had to do without a day in they lives, and now they ain't got nothin'. They gonna have a hard time. We got to pray for them, baby."

Jane Ellen did pray, both alone and with Mama, and while she believed God could intervene, she didn't really expect it to happen. And two weeks after arriving home for the holidays, she caught a ride to the bus station for the trip back to school with no further word from her white friend.

For the first time ever, Jane Ellen was glad to return to A and M in early January. Christmas holidays had been the most depressing since early childhood. Mama had tried to "play the Pollyanna game,'" she called it, and put on a happy face, but Jane Ellen knew her grandmother better. Mama's old heart was broken.

The family had gone about their customary rituals of attending church services together, exchanging gifts, and eating a huge lunch Christmas day, with both her aunts bringing food to add to the feast Mama had worked on for days. But the chocolate pies she and Mama had baked, as usual, for Miss Pat and Mr. George sat in the pie safe until the thick meringue became weepy, and Mama had thrown them out when she thought Jane Ellen wasn't looking.

The Saturday of Lynn's scheduled wedding, Jane Ellen stayed in her small dorm room bed all day and cried most of it. She was so glad that the latest of her roommates was spending the weekend with her boyfriend and his family. Uncle Jack had written her, through Mama's dictation, that Lynn's plans had been stepped up, and the marriage was to take place during spring break. Mama had said she figured Zell decided he'd better turn the screws, or Lynn might back out. Once again, Jane Ellen mourned the lack of control that seemed the birthright of all females.

Knowing that Mama was now without a job and probably needed the extra income, Miss Hattie, Zell's mother, had hired her to help get the house ready for all the festivities, and Mama had gone, avoiding Mr. Till, Zell's evil father, whenever possible. Because Lynn's parents had no permanent address, the Green home would serve as the center for all the bridal activities.

The gifts would be displayed there, and the bridesmaids' luncheon would also be held there. Curtains had to be starched and ironed. Floors had to be scrubbed and waxed. Rugs had to be beaten and turned. Crocheted tablecloths and doilies had to be soaked in bluing. Closets had to be cleaned. Beds had to be readied for out-of-town guests. Contents of the pantry had to be catalogued and updated. The refrigerator and two freezers had to be defrosted and restocked. Mama, Miss Hattie, and Essie Lou, Miss Hattie's regular house girl, worked for two weeks solid on the preparations.

Three of Lynn's sorority sisters and a cousin from Jackson, Mississippi, were to be Lynn's wedding attendants. Mama had gone into great detail about their dresses, Lynn's gown and veil, and all the activity. Jane Ellen thought her heart would break when she read the words of the letters from Mama in Uncle Jack's handwriting.

Jane Ellen was so sad because she knew Lynn was entering into a loveless marriage with a man she didn't even like, and she was sad because the mores of the day made it impossible for Jane Ellen to be a part of her best friend's wedding. She knew that she and Lynn had shared more than Lynn and her Alpha Gamma Delta sisters ever could, and the cousin from Mississippi was practically a stranger. So Jane Ellen stayed in bed all day and cried for Lynn and for her own loss. And to her chagrin, pouted with Mama for being in Mr. Till's house.

When Jane Ellen got home for her own spring break a week and a half after the wedding, she learned from Mama that Lynn and Zell would be living in the house with his parents. Because Mr. Till was getting on in years and was in poor health, Zell had taken over the management of his family's store. She could only imagine how the black population felt about that!

Chapter II

Jane Ellen could barely remember a time when she and Lynn had not been best friends. They had been only four and five years old when Fate brought them together.

"Jane Ellen, it's Papa. He's dead. Mr. Till Green shot him at the store and hauled the body home. You can't go in there. Mama don't want you seein' him," her Aunt Sami sobbed from the porch and sent her back down the path to Uncle Jack's where earlier she had been playing with Jimmi and Pie. She met Uncle Jack running up the path toward Mama and Papa's—now just Mama's.

Her beloved Papa, the kindest, gentlest person she had ever known was gone. Gone before she could ever tell him how much she loved him, respected him, depended on him to make her wise and decent like he was. Gone before she was old enough or experienced enough to know these were things she felt. And all over a stupid, arrogant white man's need to affirm his worth through the barrel of a gun.

All the Klansmen and wannabees who lived in the Bottom—only two generations past sharecropping—would rant and rave for weeks about poor old Till. They would declare how that sorry nigger wronged the white man by overstepping his bounds. They would sleep better knowing that a superior man with skin darker than theirs had died before he could threaten their position in the caste system that was the South of the '50s.

In addition to the rednecks, the old Southern aristocrats had to embrace their own and pretend to believe that Till was right and that Old Stump had truly done what he was accused of doing. The women doubted; Miss Hattie knew, but she couldn't tell. Her lifestyle and that of her only child depended on her silence.

She came by to pay her respects to the family whose patriarch was dead at the hand of her husband, with son Zell in tow.

The boy's left eye had a yellowish green bruise over it, indicating it was well on its way to healing as he held Miss Hattie's hand and strolled by Papa's plain pine casket, a casket that could not be opened because there wasn't enough of a head left to piece together.

Miss Hattie had been by the house earlier on Sunday, two days after Papa's death, and had spent over an hour alone with Mama in the back room. Through the thin walls, Jane Ellen listened as amid Mama's wails and sobs, the girl heard Miss Hattie's soothing voice in an attempt to reassure Mama that everything would be all right. They would be "taken care of," whatever that meant.

How could anybody ever take care of them the way Papa had? He provided their physical needs with his job at Mr. Till's store. More than that, he provided emotional support and her conduit for knowledge. He was the one who held her on his lap and read to her from his big Bible. He had been teaching her the characters, beginning with Adam and Eve. They had just finished talking about Daniel, and Papa had laughed at her pronunciations of Shadrach, Meshach, and Abednego. There were lots of characters yet to be discussed, and Mama couldn't read. What was an inquisitive child to do without someone to teach her such things? How did Miss Hattie possibly think they could be taken care of with Papa gone?

Now lost in her reverie over the Sunday's visit by Miss Hattie, she was shocked when she looked up from the head of Papa's casket in the front room and saw Zell turn back at the door, catch her eye, and give her the finger. She had watched, terrified, as Uncle Jack slapped Pie off the bench at the dinner table one day when her cousin had raised his index finger at Jimmi, his sister. She didn't know what it meant and wasn't sure Pie knew, but she was certain he would never do it again. Zell smiled now as he raised his left hand high so there could be no doubt as to his intent. That same sinister smile she had seen on his father's face when she went into his store stared back at her now. Why? She had never done anything to the boy.

After that first visit, Miss Hattie had been true to her word. The rations that had been a part of Papa's pay at the store had kept coming, and apparently were even increased; although, at the time Jane Ellen had been too young to calculate such things.

Miss Hattie and Zell drove the groceries and other staples out to the house in a shiny new Cadillac. Jane Ellen always tried to stay close to Mama's side and to avoid contact with the boy on those visits. For the first two months, Mama accepted the provisions without any objections. On the first Saturday of the third month, however, Mama got all dressed up and waited on the pretty beige plastic-covered couch Papa had bought on credit less than six months earlier. When Miss Hattie's baby blue guzzler stirred the dust on the dirt road, Mama went to the door and stood until Zell got out with the first of the boxes.

Mama held the door open for him, invited Zell in, and asked him to wait inside while she went outside to talk to his mama. Mama left the house, ignorant of the earlier encounter between the two children, and Jane Ellen was left to face her tormentor alone.

Jane Ellen, too short to reach the stove, was standing on tiptoe, stirring a pot of greens as her grandmother had instructed when Zell entered the kitchen door. And although she had her back to him, she could sense his presence as the hair on the back of her neck stood on end.

He slammed the box he was carrying onto the table, startling her and causing her to turn around, as he strode toward her with that same evil smile she had once seen before, at Papa's casket.

"Hey, nigger, what you cookin'? Possum? Ain't that what nigger gals supposed to do? Cook possum and make babies? Daddy says that's all ya'll good for. Wanna try to make a baby while the possum's cooking? We could go out back. You got a barn? Daddy says niggers always ready for a roll in the hay. And don't try to tell me you're too young, gal. Niggers are born knowin' what to do."

For the second time Jane Ellen understood nothing of what the mean spirited Zell actually meant by words that made no sense to her, but she understood the hate with which he spat them at her, and she was afraid. With her back now to the stove, Jane Ellen reached behind her and wrapped a wee hand around the wooden handle of the butcher knife Mama had used earlier that day to chop the pork now seasoning the collard greens. It was the knife they called "The Knife" because it had always been kept sharp at Papa's insistence so that he could slice tomatoes and onions easily at the table. At the moment she grabbed "The Knife," Mama reentered the kitchen door with another of the grocery boxes. Zell looked up at the woman, smiled, and left the way he had come, but not before he had turned back and winked at the frightened little girl who had no idea of what she could possibly have done to evoke such strong feelings in someone who didn't even know her.

Besides, it was Zell's daddy who had killed her Papa. Shouldn't she be the one who was mad, not him? She was mad aplenty, but what good was it? She couldn't do anything about it. She didn't even have anybody she could tell how mad and frightened she was.

Chapter III

The light was burning on the back porch of the big white house when she and Mama arrived, just a little after daybreak, and Miss Pat met them as they reached the top step. She smiled and invited them in. Jane Ellen cowered behind Mama's long skirt in an effort to hide, but the yellow-haired young woman peeked around the large black woman and introduced herself to the frightened, angry, most private little girl. Jane Ellen recognized her as one she had seen with her own little girl in town, but they had never spoken before. The lady was so pretty and now spoke so softly, Jane Ellen was afraid she was going to like her, and wasn't she one of *them*?

Mama and Miss Pat planned the details of Mama's work schedule as the three of them toured the house. That is, the house with the exception of the upstairs bathroom where a weak baritone voice could be heard in an even weaker rendition of a Hank Williams tune as the vocalist showered. They also did not enter what Miss Pat referred to as "the baby's room," the bedroom at the end of the upstairs hallway.

The house was from a fairy tale — so big and white with no newspapers glued to the walls as insulation in any room. Nowhere could Jane Ellen smell the musty scent of an open flame or of kerosene as she had in every house she had ever entered before today. And the fresh, distinct aroma of each separate room was her first introduction to this alien environment and the first recollection she conjured up later when she remembered this day.

Following their quick tour, Miss Pat directed them back to the kitchen as she showed Mama the locations of all the supplies; then she left grandmother and young charge alone as she vanished upstairs. Jane Ellen sat at the large rectangular oak table as Mama cooked bacon, scrambled eggs, and prepared grits, pancakes, and buttermilk biscuits as her new boss had instructed. The smells blending with that of the coffee gurgling in the percolator prompted the girl's mouth to water. She had never smelled so many good things prepared for the morning meal. She and Mama usually had either buttered grits or biscuits with syrup—never both, and coffee and meat were reserved for Sunday mornings and special occasions only. All this food was alluring, and she asked Mama if she could eat. The resounding "no" was not so strong a deterrent as the harsh look her grandmother shot her. She didn't understand why she couldn't eat but understood perfectly that now was no time to ask for an explanation. Instead she began setting the food on the table as instructed.

Miss Pat and a man Jane Ellen had also seen around town came into the room just as she was putting the plate of hot biscuits out. They were laughing, and his arm draped over her shoulder. Jane Ellen had never seen such a display of affection between adults before. She knew that Papa and Mama had loved each other, but she never saw them touch, and the word "love" had never been exchanged between them in her presence.

The smiling man walked to Jane Ellen's position beside Mama at the stove and extended his hand. "You must be Jane Ellen. Your grandfather told me a lot about you. Said you were something of a Bible scholar. Your grandfather was a good man. I thought a lot of him, and I hope you and I can be friends."

"Macy," the man addressed Mama, "everything smells delicious! I can't wait; I'm as hungry as a bear!"

Jane Ellen liked this big white man. That bothered her because she felt she was being unfaithful to Papa's memory. But he said he had liked Papa, and he treated her like she was grown up and somebody. Gosh! He had shaken her hand! And besides, Papa must have liked him, too; he had told Mr. George about their Bible studies. Staying mad and hating were so hard to do, she discovered.

Mr. George and Miss Pat sat down and began filling their plates, but only after he had blessed the food and each of them, asking divine guidance for all for the day. Papa used to ask God's blessings each day, too. This *was* a good man; she could tell.

The ooh's and ah's over the meal lasted throughout breakfast, and Jane Ellen watched Mama as nervousness gave way to pride. Maybe this arrangement wouldn't be *so* bad, after all. Right now, though, Jane Ellen just longed for syrup and a biscuit with a cold glass of milk. That much she could have had at home. She was certain she was going to sit in the midst of all this plenty and starve to death!

Just as Miss Pat and Mr. George were finishing their second cup of coffee, there was a flutter outside the kitchen door, and Lynn Wambles burst in with a scruffy mongrel nipping at her heels. Her blond hair was still tousled from the night's sleep, and she wore a pale pink gown and no shoes, even though the early September morning was a bit cool. She ran to her father, climbed into his lap, and rubbed her cheek against his. "Daddy, I'm so glad you've already shaved. I don't like it when you're scratchy." Father and daughter joined in a childlike giggle.

Jane Ellen watched this exchange from across the room and ached for Papa, but not for long. The disheveled little girl spied her in the corner, jumped from her father's lap, and raced to face her.

"Hi, my name's Lynn . Who are you, and why are you here so early?"

Miss Pat hurried and scooped her up, admonishing her for the lack of manners. "Lynn, this is Jane Ellen Robbins and her grandmother, Mrs. Macy Robbins. Mrs. Robbins is responsible for this wonderful breakfast your daddy and I just enjoyed. She'll be working for us every weekday for a while, and maybe Jane Ellen can come along with her and play with you, but only if you can remember to be polite. Right now, go wash your face, brush your hair and teeth, and get dressed for breakfast. You two girls can eat and get to know each other better."

"Oh, good!" Lynn squealed. "She can be my new best friend!" With that she grabbed Jane Ellen's hand and pulled her along.

If Jane Ellen thought the rest of the house was from a fairy tale, Lynn's room must be from heaven. Everything was pink and white, and toys filled every inch of floor space. There were dolls, stuffed animals, books, and on a table in the corner rested a tiny white tea set adorned with pink roses. A one-eyed bear and Raggedy Ann sat in the two chairs drawn up to the table. As Lynn hurriedly dressed and brushed her hair, Jane Ellen tried to assimilate all this, but there was too much to take in. When Lynn scooted though a door at the back of the bedroom and started running water in the sink in her bathroom, Jane Ellen thought she must be dreaming. This child, scarcely larger than she, had her own bathroom! The only bathroom for the little house at the bottom of the hill was a two-seater toilet out back, shared by her household and that of Uncle Jack.

When her new friend emerged moments later with a glistening face and fresh breath, the two girls again held hands as they hurried back to the kitchen. Mama had cleared the table of dirty dishes and had set two smaller plates for them. A glass of milk for each also waited. As the two girls ate, Lynn talked unceasingly, and Jane Ellen thought that Mama's cooking had never tasted so good.

The next morning and every morning after that, a child-sized chair waited beside the stove where the young girl could sit and talk quietly to Mama while she cooked and could wile away the time until her slightly older playmate arose and made Jane Ellen a part of the enchanted daily routine.

On weekends, Jane Ellen still played with Pie and Jimmi sometimes, but no play was like that with Lynn Monday through Friday. The two girls never tired of each other, and the white child never acted as if the black child was any different except for the first week, when she tentatively touched tightly-woven, curly hair and rubbed her hand over a dark arm. Then she laughed softly and said, "Your skin is so smooth. I wish mine felt like that."

The little black child had then reached to touch the blond hair. She giggled at its texture and mused, "How you curl that? Ain't no fireplace to heat the iron in."

Lynn showed her the pink foam rollers Mother had her sleep in every Saturday night. She even showed Jane Ellen how to put her own short hair around the twisters. It pulled, and Jane Ellen was glad she didn't have to sleep in them. She promised herself not to wiggle so much when Mama curled her hair next Saturday.

Chapter IV

The two girls were inseparable for a year, until the older Lynn started school, leaving behind her lonely playmate. That first day apart was the saddest Jane Ellen had experienced since Papa's death. The two girls still had breakfast together, but then Lynn climbed into the car with her mother who drove her the four miles to the only white school in the area. Jane Ellen spent her days helping Mama and playing with Spitz, the mongrel, nagging Mama about Lynn's afternoon arrival time.

At 3:10 each afternoon, give or take a few minutes, Miss Pat drove Lynn back, and the two girls shared a snack and the events of the day. Lynn now had new friends, but she affirmed often that the two of them were still best friends.

This became their new routine, and it was a pleasant one until another year passed, and Jane Ellen also started school.

She still walked to the big house with Mama each morning and shared breakfast with Lynn before walking alone back down the hill and across the pasture to the one-room schoolhouse where she would spend the first six years of her formal education.

Miss Cain probably tried to teach each of the students, grades one through six, but she was obviously ill equipped. Jane Ellen already knew how to read, a ready pupil to school marm Lynn, and was bored with the slow pace. She often found herself daydreaming and staring out a window. She tried to enter into the discussions with the older children but soon learned her autocratic teacher would have no part of it.

Miss Cain yelled at her and whacked her knuckles quite often. That she was "uppity" was the only explanation given for the frequent reprimands, and while Jane Ellen didn't understand what the term meant, she knew it must be bad because it was always stated with a sneer and always after she had corrected some error Miss Cain had made in pronouncing a word or working a problem in arithmetic.

Each afternoon Jane Ellen bolted from her desk and headed back up the hill to share food and the day's doings with Lynn. Jane Ellen's school experiences certainly weren't much compared to her friend's, who complained of the yucky cafeteria food while Jane Ellen remembered her sandwich and apple brought from home and consumed under the only tree in the schoolyard. Lynn giggled about that awful Buddy Smith who peeked into the girls' bathroom until Mrs. Dorn, the principal, caught him, tanned his hide, and made him chink the hole. Jane Ellen thought of her swift trips to the outhouse in the rain and how she prayed daily to be able to make it back to the big house before having to go.

Lynn raved about Halloween carnivals, school assemblies, field trips to the Little White House of the Confederacy in Montgomery and the Coca Cola Bottling Company in Selma, P.T.A. programs, and cupcakes provided each month by room mothers. Jane Ellen had no such events to share. She went to school at 8:00 each morning, got out at 3:00 each afternoon and did nothing but reading, writing, arithmetic, a little science, and a little history before, during, or after. She participated in no extracurricular activities because there were none.

Still Jane Ellen felt no resentment toward her friend, and Lynn felt no sense of superiority toward her. This was the world they lived in, and neither of them questioned it nor ever expected it to be different. Then a young minister named Martin Luther King began speaking out against such inequities, and things began to change.

Blacks talked about voting and even about attending white schools. Mama was totally opposed and declared it was just "high fallotin' colored folks gettin' rich and famous at the expense of pore colored folks." Aunt Sami and her husband believed otherwise. They loaded their whole family into Uncle Jack's old pickup truck and drove to Montgomery to hear Dr. King speak. They tried to get Mama, Jane Ellen, and Uncle Jack and his family to go, too, but Uncle Jack had to work, and Mama refused in no uncertain terms. And anybody who knew Mama knew better than to argue with her when she made up her mind. So Jane Ellen had to endure Janese and Denese, Aunt Sami's twins, and their rantings and ravings about their trip to see their new savior. Jane Ellen hated them for their excitement and resented Mama for making it impossible for her to share it. She couldn't even discuss this new turn of events—certainly not with Mama whose close-mindedness prevented it or with Lynn whose skin color made it impossible. Jane Ellen just seethed and once again hated the lack of control in her own life.

When she was frustrated, angry, or depressed, she wondered how things would have been different if she had been reared by her parents. Daddy had been Mama and Papa's youngest and apparently the favorite, if Aunt Sami's and Uncle Jack's stories of their brother were even close to the truth.

Mama said Daddy was independent and a dreamer. Aunt Sami said he was rebellious and lazy. They all agreed, however, that he was handsome. Muh Dear had been a looker, too. Daddy had met her after she moved to Alabama from Detroit to live with her grandparents when she was a high school junior. Daddy was a senior and a jock. The two became an item immediately when Muh Dear, according to Mama, set her cap for Daddy.

They ran away and married the next summer, and Jane Ellen arrived eleven months later. Muh Dear never finished high school, and the young couple spent their short marriage in the little house with Mama and Papa. Aunt Sami and Uncle Jack were both already married and out of the house by that time, but there was a great deal of tension in those four small rooms. Mama didn't like the light-skinned girl, and Jane Ellen guessed she had done nothing to make her daughter-in-law feel welcome in their home.

Six months after their daughter's birth, Ellie Broadnax Robbins caught the bus back to Detroit and never returned to Alabama. Mama took over the infant's care, and Daddy went back to his independent or rebellious ways, according to who related the story. Eight months later, his family buried him, the result of a Saturday night ride with two of his old football buddies, who also died in the wreck.

All of this background Jane Ellen learned in bits and pieces from her family. She knew no other parents but Mama and Papa, and her aunt and uncle and their four children were her siblings. She had never even seen a picture of her mother but had memorized every distinguishing feature of her father as captured in his light oil senior portrait, proudly displayed by Mama over the fireplace in the living room.

Although some of Muh Dear's cousins that Jane Ellen saw at school had told her there were two half brothers and a half sister in Detroit, Jane Ellen never had any desire to meet them. Muh Dear had been "fast" according to the people Jane Ellen loved, and not a good mother. But sometimes after Papa died, Jane Ellen dreamed of a beautiful young woman holding her, caressing her, and singing lullabies to her, and she would awaken crying. Mama fed her, clothed her, and loved her, but never held her or expressed any warmth toward her. Mama was too strong for that. So the little black girl with no parents wished her Muh Dear hadn't been fast, that her Daddy hadn't been so independent, and once again that the white man with the evil smile hadn't killed Papa. The warmth in her existence now came from her life as a part of the Wambles household.

Chapter V

Through sixth grade, Jane Ellen had no close friends but Lynn. They had breakfast and an afternoon snack together each school day. During the long, hot summer days, they shared two meals five days a week and spent many lazy afternoons lying on their backs, sinking into the lush pale green of Lynn's bedroom carpet. The window air conditioning unit rustled the white organdy curtains and stirred the pale pink floral bedspread on the white four-poster bed. Innocent white girl of privilege and innocent black girl of poverty (who didn't give a whit about their differences) giggling, discussing life, making career plans, or just deciding what light mischief they would get into later. Perhaps they might sneak into Miss Pat's closet and play dress-up, or they might "play like" they were driving Miss Pat's car to Montgomery. One time that game didn't go so well, and Miss Pat's car ended up in the muddy ditch beside the driveway. That incident their "driving."

Saturdays Lynn spent shopping with her mother, going to birthday parties, having her hair done, riding her pony, or helping Mr. George with light chores of their large estate. With more than two thousand acres of rich Black Belt land, Mr. George had as many as fifteen farm hands, and her help was of little consequence. He just loved having her around, and she loved sharing the time with her hard working father. To say Mr. George doted on this lovely only child could not begin to convey his adoration; he practically worshipped her.

She was perfection in his eyes, and he recognized in her a combination of the best physical, moral, emotional, and intellectual qualities of him and his dear wife. He absolutely couldn't get enough of Lynn.

Saturdays at Jane Ellen's small wood frame house were spent with Mama -sweeping yards until not a speck of debris could be found by even Mama's omnipotent eye, washing in the old cast iron pot under the wash shed, ironing with a flat iron heated in the fireplace, or cooking on the wood-burning stove. Water had to be hauled from the faucet in Uncle Jack's back yard, and while it was only a quarter of a mile's walk, it could be quite a frigid trip on a cold January morning for a careless little girl if she tipped the bucket on the way home.

As she grew, chopping wood was added to Jane Ellen's list of chores. Papa had done it after work and on Sundays. Sometimes now Pie would help with the woodpile, but most weekends he made extra money breaking Mr. George's green colts. Pie was wiry and agile, like Papa, a perfect combination for riding the young, unbroken horses. Chopping wood could, like hauling water, be a chilly chore during the winter months, but in the summer it was welcome relief from the oppressive heat inside the tiny house. And there were considerably more hot than cold days in the Deep South.

Any spare time on Saturdays would find Jane Ellen at Uncle Jack's playing with Jimmi and Pie, if he was not working with Mr. George or helping Uncle Jack. Pie was two year older than Jane Ellen; Jimmi was three months younger. Seldom did either of the three play with Aunt Sami's girls who were a year younger than Jane Ellen.

The twins had always struck Jane Ellen as downright ignorant, much like their father, Uncle Bud, whom she didn't like very much. Nobody in the family did, except Aunt Sami. Mama said he was from across the swamp, and nothing good came from the lower side of that bog. Even the disease-causing mosquitoes had their home there, according to

Mama. She had not approved of Sami's "marrying down" and had never tried to hide the fact. She told Aunt Laura Mae, Uncle Jack's wife, that his head was no bigger than a hickory nut, obviously no room for a brain in there. Jane Ellen, Pie, and Jimmi had overhead that observation through a door and had to bury their faces in Mama's mattress so their giggles wouldn't reach the kitchen and send Mama scurrying for the strop, that great castigator of disobedient and disrespectful children.

Sundays also found Jane Ellen and Lynn in separate worlds. Lynn and her parents dressed in their finery, and Mr. George drove them, in the Cadillac, to the Baptist Church for Sunday school. Every fourth Sunday they stayed for worship service. The first three Sundays of each month they left after Sunday school to attend services at the Methodist, Episcopal, and Presbyterian churches respectively. None of the churches with such small congregations could afford a full-time minister; so each denomination joined the others when they "had preaching." Returning home by noon, the family had either roast beef or fried chicken and vegetables that Miss Pat prepared for Sunday dinner. (Lunch" wasn't a word Southerners used, except in reference to the midday meal at school). Sunday afternoons were for visiting friends and relatives, sharing *The Montgomery Advertiser*, or riding horses on the estate.

Jane Ellen and Mama also dressed in their best attire each Sunday morning and caught on with Uncle Jack and his family to ride his pick-up truck to the African Methodist Episcopal Church. Aunt Sami, Uncle Bud, and the twins also rode with them most Sundays. The children always piled into the back; sometimes the overflow of adults from the cab also joined them in the rear. There was an old chenille bedspread lining the floor to protect their starched clothes. During the winter, a stiff, army green tarpaulin thrown over them staved off some of the chill.

Sunday school at the AME Church began at eleven with preaching at noon. Services could last until four in the afternoon, and Jane Ellen made sure she ate at least one or two of Mama's biscuits with plenty of ham, sausage, or bacon and syrup before leaving home. When they finally got back to the house, Mama would rewarm greens, peas, or some kind of beans, fried chicken or pork chops kept fresh in the icebox, and biscuits left from breakfast. There was often bread pudding or egg custard, too. The conversation was usually light and of little consequence, but occasionally politics or other controversial issues came up, and then Mama's conservatism often clashed with the modern thinking of her only daughter and her family. Nobody ever left the table mad; nobody left with a change of thinking either. The entire family always shared this meal, and it was the highlight of Jane Ellen's week. Years later when she was far from home, it was about that time each Sunday that she found herself homesick.

After sixth grade, Jane Ellen's life took another turn. She no longer walked to school but caught a bus at the crossroads cattle gap for the fifteen-mile trip to the nearer of the two black high schools in the county. She no longer had time to walk up the hill to Lynn's each morning. She usually had a cold biscuit and a glass of milk for breakfast because Mama was already at the big house when Jane Ellen dressed, but each afternoon she did return to the cozy kitchen where the two girls established a new routine in their conjoined lives.

As they had their cookies and milk or peanut butter and jelly sandwiches, they entertained Mama and Miss Pat with their scholastic goings on. Jane Ellen liked her new school much better than the first feeble attempt at education.

Her classes were larger because students were bussed from a large surrounding area and a dozen other schools like Miss Cain's. There was movement between classes, and grade levels were separated in different rooms. There was even a cafeteria. Jane Ellen no longer had to carry her pail. Lunch cost a quarter each day, and while money was scarce, Mama always managed to have it waiting on Jane's orange crate dressing table each morning. There was never any spare change, but she had no need of any. Miss Pat bought her school supplies when she bought Lynn's, and Jane Ellen had the nicest notebooks, pens, pencils, and books at her school. There were no vending machines for snacks. Food for recess had to be brought from home.

For six years, Jane Ellen never brought anything to eat; she was so happy to be free of the lunch pail. Besides, recess was usually spent with Mrs. Smith, the librarian, soaking up all the knowledge she could in the ill-equipped facility. It was a Mecca for her eager, intelligent mind.

Beginning in Jane Ellen's eighth grade year, Mrs. Smith made her a library assistant, and for a class period each day for five years she was allowed to catalog, check in, check out, re-cover, and lovingly handle the two hundred three novels, one set of World Book encyclopedia, one unabridged dictionary, and twenty-two biographies comprising the library in a black school in a poor county in the Alabama of the sixties. She never imagined that any library could hold more volumes. By the time she graduated in 1966 with a 99.8 average, she had read all the novels, all the biographies, and had done at least one report a week from the encyclopedia. The biographies of Abraham Lincoln, George Washington Carver, and Helen Keller had been read three times each and had all been shared word for word with Mama.

Jane Ellen's social life still revolved around her relationship with Lynn, but there were other interests as well, now. She was active in student government, held leadership positions in academic organizations, and showed even a slight interest in boys. The basketball and football players who appealed to most of her schoolmates didn't interest her. She was attracted to those few men who, like her, longed for a fuller life through academic enlightenment.

With trouble brewing in an isolated spot on the globe called Viet Nam, the really intelligent young men pushed the scholastic limits during their senior year. They needed to excel enough for a scholarship because none of the parents could afford to send their children to college. Higher education was their only way to guarantee deferment from the military draft.

Jane Ellen had other reasons for academic excellence. She loved to learn. The minutest bit of knowledge was to be savored and assimilated. Her years at Paul Lawrence Dunbar High School were idyllic. She never missed a day, was never late to class, and never made less that an "A." The day she graduated, May 27, 1966, all of her family, Miss Pat, Mr. George, and Lynn (home from college for the occasion) heard her optimistic valedictory address and rejoiced with her when she was awarded a full academic scholarship to Alabama Agricultural and Mechanical School in Normal, Alabama, near Huntsville. After the program, the family returned to Mama's house and gathered around the table for another meal of her favorite foods and conversation devoted solely to Jane Ellen and her future. Life couldn't get any better.

A year earlier, Lynn had left home for the University of Alabama where sororities were well established, and old money felt compelled to send their young. Letters arrived weekly addressed to Jane Ellen and Mama, and their beloved blond beauty shared every aspect of her collegiate life. In return, Jane Ellen sent a chronology of their lives each week. When Lynn came home on weekends, she always made it a point to see Mama and Jane Ellen, and during summers spent at home, the two girls again often gathered around the kitchen table of the big house.

Social changes were occurring in rapid succession—the Selma to Montgomery Civil Rights March, the assassination of white activist Viola Liuzzo, the murder of a priest dedicated to the cause. All these occurred within spitting distances of the homes of Lynn and Jane Ellen. Farther away, Dr. Martin Luther King, President John Kennedy and his brother Bobby lost their lives to assassins' bullets. Alabama's Governor George Wallace stood in the schoolhouse door in Tuscaloosa to prevent the University's integration.

Yet it was understood when blacks and whites occupied the same premises that these subjects were off limits for discussion.

Jane Ellen had such mixed feelings about the events. She loved Mama and knew the old lady's sentiments, and she loved Lynn, but she couldn't help but wonder if the activists might be at least partially right. It did seem silly and wasteful to support dual systems, and the murders were wrong. Nevertheless, her life would not be affected appreciably by the changes, she thought; she tried not to dwell on them.

Chapter VI

From the first Christmas of Mama's employ, the Wambles family had showered gifts on both Jane Ellen and her grandmother. Jane Ellen loved dolls, and she had a collection of Madame Alexander beauties identical to that of Lynn's, garnered through the years. She could never play with them. They were for admiring only. When she left for college, she made sure the protective covers were intact. She did have one doll unlike any of Lynn's—a black one Miss Pat had given her for her sixth birthday. It was dressed in a lovely pink gingham dress and white pinafore with white patent leather shoes. Before then she hadn't known there were black dolls. Sally, as Jane Ellen named her, was for playing, not just for admiration. It was from observing that gorgeous creature that Jane Ellen first determined that black was beautiful, long before she ever heard the catch phrase.

Jane Ellen and Mama always cooked something special or worked with Uncle Jack and Pie to craft wooden gifts for Mr. George, Miss Pat, and Lynn at Christmas and on birthdays.

After both girls left for college, the gift exchange continued although the dolls for both girls ceased. In their stead were expensive blouses, sweaters, coats, handbags, and fragrances, always wrapped in exquisite paper from the most elite shops in Montgomery. Jane Ellen could smell the luxury of the store in the tissue. She always saved the boxes and caught furtive sniffs periodically after the new had worn off the gift itself. She carried at least one of the boxes back to A & M each

January for just that purpose. It made her feel special and loved on days when she was just a poor, lonely young lady trying valiantly to get a good education in spite of the weak background she brought from her inadequate elementary and high school experience.

Many nights during her freshman year she got only one or two hours' sleep because there was so much material that she had never seen before, things that many of her classmates took for granted. There was also the necessity of her job in the school's cafeteria which bit into her sleep time. She had to be on the serving line at six thirty each weekday morning. Any free time was spent in teaching herself facts that her teachers assumed all incoming students already knew.

She heard the girls in her dorm exchanging stories of partying, drinking, doing drugs, and making out in the parking lots, but she had neither time nor patience for such. None of that was college to her; college was learning and doing her best. She knew she was considered a snob and a prude; she had heard those discussions, too. But the opinions of those small-minded childish girls did not bother her one bit.

She never really got to know any of her roommates. She had a different one each year because they all requested to be moved. She didn't care about being their friend; so she didn't care that none of them wanted to be hers. It wasn't that she disliked them; she just didn't choose to know them.

She wrote to Mama each week, addressing the letters to Uncle Jack. She knew he and Mama cherished their time together as he read about a life none of them back home could imagine. Mama had never gone to school at all, and Uncle Jack had graduated from the local substandard institution. They were thrilled with Jane Ellen's progress, and Uncle Jack always slipped her a five or a ten each time she was home, in spite of his difficult time making ends meet. She was the hope of the future for the entire family.

Getting home was no easy task; Jane Ellen had to take the bus to Montgomery and then catch a ride with someone going her way. Sometimes Mama would work it out either with Mr. George or Miss Pat to meet her, and when Lynn was home from school, she sometimes met Jane Ellen at the bus depot. Because of the inconvenience and expense, Jane Ellen came home holidays and seldom in between.

Holidays at home were always joyous times of catching up on family news, absorbing community gossip, participating in church activities, enjoying Mama's good cooking, sleeping as she could never do at school, and sharing college experiences with Lynn.

The Christmas of Jane Ellen's junior year, Lynn's senior year, all her usual rides had been unable to meet her bus. So it was that she had gotten a lift from Montgomery with Mr. Bob Tate, her former Sunday school teacher, who worked at a milk processing plant in town. Mama had arranged it all.

The anticipation had been building for days, and the short auto trip home seemed eternal. She had little in common with Mr. Tate; so conversation was strained. He was nice enough; she just couldn't easily think of topics of interest to him.

Her excitement of getting home was heightened somewhat by her desire to end the boring ride. So, it was with great expectations she entered Mama's familiar door only to have her plans crushed with the most unfamiliar changes in Lynn's life.

The events of the Wambles economic fall and Lynn's predetermined future served as a catalyst for Jane Ellen's academic pursuits. Never had she been so determined to take charge of her own life in the only way she thought possible — a good education. She was certain that nobody would dictate to her how to live her life and with whom, as was the case with Lynn.

A year later, with a perfect 4.0 GPA, Jane Ellen Robbins graduated top of her class in social services. Not that she had any great love for the field. For females of the day, that was one of their three choices. Since she had absolutely no interest in nursing or teaching, she found it was expected, if not necessary, to follow that route. So she interviewed with representatives from social agencies of every sort from all regions of the country. Feeling the pull of the unknown and a need to escape the bonds of her background, Jane Ellen accepted a position with the New York City Welfare Department and for the first time in her twenty-one years, prepared to travel outside the state of Alabama.

On her last trip home before the move, Mama gave her Papa's Bible, a gift from his mother, her great grandmother, along with a short lesson on who she was.

"Jane Ellen," Mama began, "we ain't never had much, but you had opportunities nobody else in this family ever had. That means you got a responsibility, girl. Everybody lookin' to you to do good and make us proud, like you always done. Remember who you is and where you come from. Remember, too, what we stand for, and don't go thinkin' you better than yo raisin'. You Jane Ellen Robbins, a fine young lady from a fine family, but you ain't no better than nobody, just like ain't nobody better'n you. And whatever you do, don't let nobody be meddlin' with yo dream. We love you, chile, and all of us is always gon' be here for you."

It was the first time Jane Ellen had ever heard her grandmother utter the word "love," and it took her somewhat by surprise. She collapsed into Mama's ample arms, crying and holding on for her life—a familiar life that she was abandoning for the unknown one that she hoped and prayed would bring her fulfillment. Her childhood and dependency were over, and she had never felt so afraid. She was prepared intellectually, she believed, but socially she knew she wasn't ready. She had lived a sheltered existence surrounded by those she loved and who loved her. She knew she wasn't equipped to deal with many issues. Hers would be trial by fire, she feared, but she was certain she had to go.

She had precious little experience with the opposite sex. She had never even had a boyfriend. It wasn't that she hadn't had offers. She had had male friends in high school who wanted to take her out, but transportation in the rural country had been an issue, and apparently nobody had found her appealing enough to rustle up a vehicle to come calling. She had reread *A Tree Grows in Brooklyn* the night of her junior prom and had helped Mama make souse the night of her senior prom.

There had been a few dates during college, but no relationship lasting more than a couple of weeks. When they learned she wouldn't put out, not one of the boys stayed around to get to know her. Mama had taught her that her virginity was the greatest gift she could give her husband and that physical love was to be shared only between married couples. The word "sex" had never been exchanged between her and any of her family, but she knew their beliefs on the subject, and shared them. Besides, she had not met marrying material yet.

The closest male friend she ever had she had met through Lynn. Sam Thomas lived with his wife and three sons near the Bottom, where the poorest of poor whites had often settled a generation or two earlier. Donny was the oldest of the Thomas boys and a year older than Lynn. During the summers while Mr. Sam worked with Mr. George in the hay fields and with the beef cattle, Donny sometimes tagged along to the big house to do odd jobs for Miss Pat. The visits began when the boy was only eleven, but even at such a young age, he was eager and was well versed in most chores. His father apparently had taught him well.

Donny often worked under adverse conditions, too—two young girls following him around asking questions while trying most unsuccessfully to help. He was always polite;

however, and he took great pains to teach them while never slowing his pace. Miss Pat made sure the three of them had children's fare, not vegetables, the days they shared the midday meal. While she and Mr. George lunched on field peas or butter beans, the youngsters ate hot dogs, hamburgers, or ham sandwiches, all served with French fries. Ice cream was most often the dessert on those days, too. Donny ate as if he hadn't eaten since his last trip to the big house, and Mama sometimes had to cook two or three times before filling him.

Those encounters continued throughout Donny's high school years, and each of the three promised to keep in touch when he moved to Montgomery to work as a policeman following his high school graduation. He had sent both girls his address, and he and Jane Ellen exchanged numerous letters during her junior and senior years in high school and during her college days. Since he never mentioned hearing from Lynn, Jane Ellen had assumed the two of them didn't correspond, but she never asked.

When she was confused about some male in her life, it was Donny to whom Jane Ellen turned for advice, and he always asked for her opinion on important issues, as well. She was thrilled when he told her, via a rare phone call to the dorm, about Sadie, a police dispatcher he had met on the job. According to the call, he had been dating her for eight months and wanted to ask her to marry him. He wouldn't pop the question, though, until Jane Ellen approved her. So during Christmas break of her sophomore year, Donny drove out to Mama's in his old tan Volkswagen bug with its peeling paint and rust spots and picked her up for the drive to Montgomery to meet Sadie. Mama had a fit!

"Ain't no self-respectin' black girl gonna git in the car with no white boy and take off, just them two!" she admonished. "What is folks gonna think? And what kind a raisin' he had cause him to think any such a way? I liked that boy when he wadn't but a youngun and I was tryin' so to fill him up, but I shore thought he had better sense. Must be white trash. I hope y'all plannin' on takin' the back roads so nobody see you."

Jane Ellen understood her grandmother's objections, but the older woman had never understood the relationship between the two young people. There was no sexual attraction at all. They were just close childhood friends who chose to remain adult friends.

Mama was not the least bit warm and friendly when Donny arrived, and Jane Ellen worried about his being offended, but also she worried about upsetting the grandmother she loved so. But Donny laughed about his cold reception, and Jane Ellen tried to be flippant, but she never liked having Mama mad with her. She did get tickled at the reactions of some of the locals they passed on their way; some even stopped what they were doing to stare. They continued merrily on their way, however, to review poor unsuspecting Sadie whose judge and jury was on the way to determine her worth for marrying.

Because integration sometimes still didn't fit comfortably and because stares still occurred in public places, as they had verified on their drive, Donny prepared dinner for the three of them at his apartment rather than at a restaurant. Jane Ellen liked Sadie immediately; she was perfect for Donny, and there was a pang of jealousy she hated to claim. Not over Donny, but over their couple status.

On the drive back to the country, Jane Ellen teased an anxious Donny by having him think she wasn't quite sure of his choice of mates, but the ruse didn't last long. She couldn't conceal her true enthusiasm. He proposed to Sadie the next day, and she accepted. When she returned to school, Jane Ellen found a letter from the future bride waiting. In it she thanked Jane Ellen for her blessings on their union and promised to make her a part of their married life—a life that was to begin in two weeks with a trip to the county probate judge's office.

From then on the letters between the two women often replaced those between Donny and Jane Ellen, but the frequency never waned, and Donny always added his salutations. For her graduation, the young couple sent Jane Ellen a Cross pen and a leather daily planner embossed with her initials. Also included in the graduation card was a postscript announcing Sadie's first pregnancy. Jane Ellen was elated for them.

She wanted so much to share this news with Lynn but knew it was impossible. She had not seen her friend since before the bank's seizure of their property. Mama had said she was seldom spotted outside the house except for church services. She had seen her once as Lynn was going to Zell's store and said she looked awful.

"She all peeked and pale. Don't look like she bleed a drop if you was to cut her throat. She ain't nothin' but skin and bones, neither. When I seen her, I yelled to her from acrost the street, but she make out like she don't hear me. That pore girl got more troubles than she can shake a stick at. I speck she ain't seen a good day since she married that trashy boy."

Uncle Jack had heard at the sawmill that Mr. George was selling Moormans cattle feed, and he and Miss Pat were living in a small mobile home on Miss Pat's parents' property in Selma. Miss Pat hadn't been able to find a job. All of this news caused Jane Ellen great pain, and she was sure Mama was in anguish over it, too.

Chapter VII

The June day Jane Ellen left for New York, the temperature on Mama's back porch was ninety-eight. Mama and Pie drove her to Montgomery, one bulging suitcase in the back of the truck containing everything she was carrying. Tucked between the layers of clothes were a worn Bible and a sheet of tissue paper with its elegant scent faded except in her memory.

No tears were shed as she boarded the bus, but Mama and Pie walked to the street to view her face in the window as long as possible. Because finances were tight, as always, Mama had packed food for her in a brown paper bag. Only after she had ridden four hours did she open the parcel to find the cured ham and homemade biscuit along with two fried apple pies lovingly prepared by Mama and wrapped in waxed paper. Then the tears came, unexpectedly and exceedingly. The little old white lady seated beside her looked her way sympathetically but said nothing.

After riding what seemed like weeks and looking out at more landscape than she thought existed, the exhausted young graduate pulled into the bus station in Harlem and was approached immediately by her supervisor, wearing a name tag just as she had promised in her letter.

Sandra Motes was a short woman of barely five feet who must have weighed at least two hundred fifty pounds. She greeted her new charge with a bear hug and grabbed the suitcase, easily lifting it and carrying it to her old weather-beaten, faded yellow Volvo. She opened the passenger door for Jane Ellen and maneuvered her own bulky form under the steering wheel. When they pulled into the flow of traffic, the gears ground and the front lurched as Sandra propelled the reluctant vehicle.

Never had Jane Ellen imagined so many cars could be traveling in the same place at the same time. Even at nearly midnight, the streets were teeming with automobiles of all makes and appearances, and horns honking greeted them often as Sandra followed her own traffic rules during their short drive to the YMCA Jane Ellen would call home until an appropriate affordable apartment could be found.

Her first days in New York City were a blur of activity and change as Jane Ellen settled into a new schedule of work, sleep, work, sleep. She hated her room at the Y, but it was the best she could do until she had enough money for her own place. She felt alone and totally isolated.

The people she worked with were wonderful. There was not a one she didn't like. Sandra had made sure that she was welcomed into the circle of independent, industrious women at the office. They often invited her to join them for lunch or dinner, but there were no finances for that either. She was embarrassed and too proud to admit that fact. Jane Ellen brought a piece of fruit for lunch each day, and she warmed soup on a hot plate for dinner each night. Because she had to wait two weeks for her first paycheck and because she brought so little money from home, she could not afford to socialize.

When the long awaited Friday of her first paycheck arrived, Jane Ellen wanted to shout for joy! She was truly independent at last. After taxes, the check was not nearly so much as she had expected, but it was a start. During lunch break, she rushed to the bank on the corner and opened a checking and a savings account.

From their first meeting, Sandra had been her guardian and confidante. She had called her "Jane," not "Jane Ellen" that first night at the bus station, and everyone else had followed suit. She was "Jane Ellen" only in correspondence to and from home. Sandra had invited Jane out to lunch several times and had even asked her over for a home-cooked dinner, but the younger woman had declined. Jane felt she needed to become proficient at her job before she established a social life. Besides, she was self conscious of her social skills. Her upbringing had afforded her little opportunity to fold a napkin properly in her lap or to select a wine for dinner.

The neighborhood in which she lived and worked in New York reminded her of war zones she had heard her Uncle Bud describe of his days in the Korean Conflict or T.V. images from Viet Nam. Drug paraphernalia, condoms, empty liquor bottles, and other filth and debris greeted her at the office entrance and at the front door of the Y each day. She tried to block all that out and think clean thoughts, as Mama had taught. She got to know no one except those with whom she worked and them only peripherally.

She didn't know how she felt about her work. It seemed merely a means to a much greater end. She wanted a place of her own and money to have the basics of life; so she went every day and did the best she could. According to her first evaluation at the end of six months, she had done an exemplary job. She got rave reviews from both Sandra and the office manager, Sandra's boss. She had empathy for the people whose sordid lives and rotten luck brought them to her for assistance. She knew what it was like to be poor and in need. She did not, however, have empathy for those who came back repeatedly for assistance because they were merely unwilling to help themselves. She had no point of reference for understanding their situation. She tried not to be abrupt and brusque when dealing with those clients, but she feared her contempt and impatience sometimes showed, as hard as she tried to bury them.

On Jane's first Christmas after leaving home, there was not enough money or time to go back to Alabama. A bus trip would have consumed the greater part of her time off and all the money she had amassed. She carefully packaged the inexpensive gifts she had bought and mailed them—the first presents she had ever given that weren't homemade, and, sadly, the first she had not hand delivered.

For Mama she bought a red wool scarf to complement the black coat Miss Pat had given her two years before. For Uncle Jack she got leather work gloves for loading and unloading lumber at the sawmill. For Aunt Laura Mae, there was a box of stationery and a book of stamps for writing to her family in Georgia. For Pie, a New York Yankees baseball cap, for Jimmi, a six month's subscription to *Ebony* magazine, and for Aunt Sami and her family, a framed photograph of Dr. Martin Luther King, Jr. She felt a little bad about the last. Perhaps she should have shopped for each of them individually, but she eased her conscience when she remembered she hadn't heard a word from any of them since she had been in New York, in spite of the weekly letters she sent their way. She could count on Uncle Jack and Aunt Laura Mae to keep her abreast of what was going on in the bi-weekly accounts. Mama always sent a message, too. There was regular correspondence from Sadie, as well, keeping her posted on the pregnancy and on their lives. For them, Jane had bought a pair of yellow booties and a porcelain picture frame for the baby's first photograph.

Christmas Eve the mailman brought Jane a package from home. There was a wooden horse whittled by Pie and painstakingly painted by Uncle Jack in beautiful pale colors, a bookmark cross stitched by Jimmi, and a tin of Mama's famous syrup cookies. Jane sat in her room caressing the crafts and eating the scrumptious treats, her salty tears mingling with the sweet dough of each bite.

Because she had two days with nothing to do and nowhere to go, she decided to take a walk around the neighborhood, something she hadn't done since her arrival. It was a mere fifteen degrees; so she piled on everything she could find. In spite of the filth and degradation around her, she noted the seasonal decorations and feeble attempts at festivity, and she longed for home, family, and warm temperatures. She hadn't noticed how far she had walked until she looked around and realized she had no idea where she was going or how to get back. Reverie due to melancholy caused her to neglect notice of the path she had taken.

Her Southern clothing was no match for the bleak winter day in Harlem, and she feared she would actually freeze. Nowhere did she see anyone of whom she felt comfortable asking directions. She was sure those she met would equate her confusion for weakness and take advantage of her. So she continued walking with no idea of where she was heading nor how to return to her room. She had been walking for what seemed like hours, and the sun was lowering in the sky when she spotted a police car parked at the curb in the next block.

She practically ran to the vehicle, only to find it empty. There was no one in sight anywhere. She leaned on the automobile and began to cry for the second time that day. Just then the door in an apartment building opened in front of her, and a young black man in police uniform emerged.

Half walking, half running, he reached her and looked directly into her eyes, "What in the world is wrong with you? Why, for one thing you must be frozen. That thin coat is no protection from this wind. Come inside and let's get you warm and see if we can help."

Unable physically or mentally to protest, Jane allowed herself to be led into the open door of the apartment where an older black man and woman stood and invited her into the front room. They fussed over her, helped her out of her coat, and brought her an afghan for her legs and a cup of blistering hot coffee. She welcomed all of this and never once protested these kindnesses of perfect strangers.

After she had warmed up enough to talk, she recanted her story and asked for directions back to the Y.

"My Lord, child, you are at least ten blocks from the Y! How long had you been walking? It's a miracle you aren't dead. Where are you from, anyway, and why are you at the Y at Christmas?"

Jane told them her background and about her job. She even found herself confiding her desire for an apartment and her homesickness this her first Christmas away from her family. She couldn't believe she had revealed so much about herself to people she didn't know.

The couple introduced themselves as Mary and William Hammond, and the policeman was their grandson William III, or Bill. Bill had dropped by with their annual gift from the chief and was on his way back to the station when he had found her weeping all over his car. He offered to drive her home; it wouldn't be out of his way, he assured her. Mr. and Mrs. Hammond also insisted that she return for lunch the next day. This time she did protest, insisting that it would be much too much of an imposition, but secretly thrilled at the ideal of not only not spending the day alone but of spending it with what seemed to be such a nice family. When she determined that her protestations were useless, she relented and agreed to be there. On the way back to the Y in his squad car, Bill assured her he would pick her up at 11:00 the next morning, as he drove from his own apartment to that of his grandparents.

Somehow when she reentered her room, it didn't appear quite so small, so dingy, or so inhospitable as it had when she had left it only a short time earlier. Even the strewn Christmas package from home didn't seem nearly so depressing. That night Jane had trouble sleeping as she eagerly awaited her first Christmas day in the city.

She awakened early and made it to the communal bathroom before the other residents so she could take a leisurely shower without being disturbed or feeling rushed. She took extra time selecting just the right thing to wear. The choices among her scant wardrobe made for little decision. Nevertheless, she fussed for an hour over various combinations, finally settling on the beige wool suit and matching silk blouse she had bought for special office meetings. She thought it complemented her light skin and cinnamon eyes.

She struggled much longer than usual with her errant hair, wishing all the while that she had invested in a good cut rather than doing it herself, but it was too late to concern herself with that now. She couldn't believe she was fretting so, anyway.

About nine o'clock, she got a call on the house phone hanging on the wall outside her room. It was Sandra, trying one last time to convince Jane to spend the day with her and her extended family. Jane told her about the experience the day before and about her plans for lunch.

"Wow, I am impressed!" exclaimed Sandra. "You have been here only six months and already Prince Charming has shown up at your door or you at his, as the case may be. Whichever, it sounds promising to me. Have a great time and call me if you back out or decide you prefer to spend the day with my six rambunctious nephews and four whiny nieces rather than with a good looking man. I won't wait by the phone for your call, though. See you tomorrow."

Jane was thankful for Sandra and her concern. She really must try harder to do some things with this her first friend in New York. She was probably lonely, too.

The wait for Bill seemed endless. She couldn't decide why she was so eager for him to arrive. Just homesick? She really doubted that was the real cause. She checked her image in the mirror hanging over the bureau one last time.

When 11:00 finally came, she had become a bit nauseous and didn't know if it was due to nerves or the fact that she had eaten nothing since Mama's cooking yesterday morning. She felt better when she looked outside and saw Bill emerging from his car. He was not in uniform and looked rather dapper in his white turtleneck, tan slacks, black blazer, and dark tweed overcoat. She prayed she was dressed appropriately.

She met him at the door, and he ushered her into the black Mustang. She slid into the warmth of the leather seat. Conversation was surprisingly easy as they drove the ten blocks, and she noticed early on that he smelled good. She wasn't familiar with fragrances for men, but she knew it wasn't Old Spice of Aqua Velva, the only aftershaves Papa or Uncle Jack had ever used.

When she and Bill entered the front door of the Hammonds' apartment, the smells from the kitchen greeted her and transported her back home. She recognized the aromas of turkey, cornbread dressing, pumpkin pie, and some form of greens, and others she wasn't sure of. Mr. Hammond met the two of them, took their coats, and led them to the kitchen where Mrs. Hammond was stirring a big pot of something on the stove while conversing with a young woman seated at the table. Inexplicably, Jane felt her heart sink. This must be Bill's wife. She had just assumed....

His grandmother interrupted her thoughts with a warm greeting. "Bill, Jane, come in. I was just telling Sally here we were being joined by another displaced person. Sally is my sister's granddaughter from Mississippi. She is working here, too, and, like you, couldn't get home for the holidays. Sally, this is Jane Robbins. Jane, Sally Tompkins."

Just as she had felt her heart sink, Jane felt it soar at this news. This was Bill's cousin! She felt like kissing the stranger. Instead, she tried to listen as Mrs. Hammond explained Sally's job and understood absolutely nothing of the explanation.

Food had not tasted so good since she moved north, nor had conversation seemed so easy as Jane spent the day with this group. She could find nothing about them that didn't appeal to her. Too soon she noted that it was getting late and asked Bill if he would drive her home. Mr. and Mrs. Hammond insisted that she come back any time and made sure they had both her work and home phone numbers.

The drive back to her room was much too short, and Jane was most reluctant to return to her meager existence after meeting the Hammonds. When they pulled up to the curb in front of the Y, Bill hurriedly exited and ran to open her door before she could object. He escorted her up the steps but made no effort to come in. He assured her that he had enjoyed the day and for her to be careful where she wandered from now on. All strangers weren't as kind as his grandparents. Thanking him, Jane was turned to go inside when he yelled over his shoulder as he returned to the car, "I'll pick you up at 7:00 Saturday night for dinner and a movie, if that's all right."

"That will be fine," was her reply. She wanted to scream, run through the streets shouting, and jump for joy. Instead, she turned and walked into the building, peeking out the window like a teenager as the Mustang disappeared from view down the street.

Chapter VIII

Jane didn't know when she fell in love. Maybe it was the first time she saw Bill in uniform at his grandparents' house. Whenever it was, it was a thing of wonder and like nothing she had ever experienced before. For a year they dated, and never once did he pressure her to compromise her principles about sex. They dined, attended movies, went to church when his schedule allowed, visited his grandparents in the city and his parents in upscale New York. He even flew home with her the second year she was in town, but he never pushed.

Taking him home was a big step. His was an affluent background, and she didn't know how he would react to the poverty that was her heritage.

They drove a rental car from the airport to the country. She had insisted on a modest one, both for financial reasons and because she didn't want anybody thinking he was "uppity." The family, particularly Mama, didn't cotton to "uppity, fancy Niggers!"

She ran the gamut of emotions as he steered the car down Highway 80, following her directions. He was fascinated by the countryside, especially the black and white dairy cows grazing in the sunshine on the sixty-eight degree December day. He wanted to let the windows down and soak up the clean air. She wouldn't let him; she remembered the smell of that pastoral scene. The Holstein, or Dalmatian, cows as he chose to call them, were a lovely sight as the bovine lunched on their silage, but there was nothing lovely about the stench produced when there were so many of them. Jane didn't want to spoil the moment quite so soon with a whiff of that!

When the couple left the main highway and turned onto the county road, she felt queasy. When they left the country road for the bumpy last segment on the rutted dirt path, she felt downright sick. When they crossed the cattle gap leading to the house, she had Bill stop the car so she could throw up. Since early childhood, this had been her reaction when she was extremely nervous, scared, or excited. She was all three. Pulling up to the front, she was embarrassed by the condition of the old house. She had never seen it as she saw it now, through the critical eyes of one who is trying to impress another. It was a fleeting thought, though; she left Bill alone as she ran inside to Mama's waiting arms. The two women separated by two generations and so many miles released eighteen months' worth of emotions as they cried and hugged and then cried some more. When Jane finally broke the embrace, she looked up to see Bill standing sheepishly in the doorway, holding her new suitcase bought specifically for this trip. She introduced the two people she loved most in the world and waited anxiously to see their reactions.

Bill set down the suitcase and extended his hand. "Mrs. Robbins, I am pleased to meet you at last. For a year now I have heard your praises sung almost daily. I was expecting to see some sort of halo attached and am frankly a bit disappointed that there isn't one. I also can't wait to sample your cooking; every restaurant we've eaten in has been unfavorable compared to the outpourings of your kitchen."

Mama shook his outstretched hand, listened to his brief monologue, and hugged him like she would her own. "Boy," she said after releasing her hold, "let's get one thing straight. Ain't no Mrs. Robbins stay in this house, far as you concerned. I'm Mama. We ain't heard nothin' but how glorious you is since that day you found this chile bellowin' at yo' mama and papa's, and I was 'spectin' some kind of wonder man. But I 'spect she done exaggerated some about you to me and about me to you. So, we best get to know one another ourselves and form our own opinions."

Jane could have hugged her again; Mama was actually trying to be funny. Before she could bask in the moment too long, however, the door flung open, and Uncle Jack and his family came barreling in. There were hugs, introductions, looks of appraisal, and a barrage of questions and answers. Everyone looked great, but Jane noticed that Mama moved more slowly and gave in to her right hip more. She had been kicked by a mule when she was a teen, and it had always been her weak spot. Now she was obviously bothered quite a bit by it and could no longer conceal the pain.

Aunt Sami, Uncle Bud, and the twins came over later that evening, and once again the family sat around the table as they had done so many times before and talked incessantly, both sharing what was new here, pumping her for information about her new life, and reliving stories of their family life together.

She brought out pictures of the one-bedroom apartment she had rented two months earlier, and the home folks marveled at the fact that it was equipped with a dishwasher, trash compactor, and washer and dryer. They still believed those things were reserved for rich white folks with lots of land. When she let it slip what her monthly rent was, she thought Uncle Jack would have a heart attack!

"Can't nobody keep up that kind of payment!" he stormed. "You gonna be out on the street or back in that dump of a room you hated at the Y. Why you get so high falootin' and think you got to live so high?"

Jane had wanted to impress them, but she never meant to worry or offend them. She attempted an explanation. "It's the cheapest thing I could find in a neighborhood I'm not afraid to go to sleep in. Besides," she retorted, "my salary isn't bad.

I'm still saving some each payday. That really is not a bad price for an apartment."

She knew he wasn't convinced, and she dared not let him know how much she was making. He would have thought she was "uppity." She hoped she didn't give the impression she thought herself better now. She would have to be careful not to mention anything financial again. She knew, too, though, that letting him know she was saving money was a good move. He had learned that lesson well from Mama and Papa and would appreciate that she had, also.

Bill went home with Uncle Jack's family to share Pie's bed that night. He crawled into the back as if he had been riding an old pick-up truck all his life. There simply was no other arrangement that would work. Mama's house was much too small, and everyone would have been uncomfortable. This was a patient man she loved. She prayed his patience wouldn't run out.

Christmas morning, Jane was as excited as she had been as a child. She awake to the aroma of ham and coffee and snuggled back under the quilts for a few more minutes, just to relish the moment and to remember every detail for future reference. When she did arise and enter the kitchen, she heard Mama singing as she knew her grandmother did when she was happy. It was so good to be home with familiar smells, familiar sounds, and family. She eased up behind Mama, grabbed her around her waist, and squeezed. Then she proceeded to scramble eggs, check the biscuits already baking in the oven, and stir the grits bubbling on the front unit. She made a mental note to buy some grits and take them back to New York where no store stocked them.

Soon she heard the distinctive sound of Uncle Jack's old truck and laughter and animated conversation as Bill led the way into the kitchen.

"Jane, I have not slept a wink." began Bill with a wink. "Pie has apparently not cut his toenails since you left home and insisted on sticking them in my legs all night. Plus, he moaned some woman's name in his sleep. I was scared he'd mistake me for her. I haven't closed my eyes all night."

An embarrassed Pie was quick to defend himself. "Ain't a word of that so, Jane Ellen. This fool makin' all that up as he go 'long. He asleep time his head hit the pillow. He had to be shook to wake him up so we could get over heah this morning."

Jane saw the good-natured grins exchanged between the two and knew they had hit it off.

After the best tasting breakfast of her life, Jane helped Mama clear the table and begin the final preparations for the big lunch they would eat at noon. The turkey that had been baked yesterday was wrapped in foil and waiting on the back stoop where it had been placed to keep it cool since the refrigerator was already overflowing. Jane remembered the year Mama went out to the stoop to get the turkey only to find the carcass Pie's dog had left when he enjoyed his early holiday meal. That was the only time she had ever heard Mama cuss, but she had called that cur something besides a creature of God that day. She could still remember, too, Papa's deep, calm voice as he admonished her.

"Macy, that dog just doin' what comes natural to it. I speck you ought to a thought about that animal 'fore you put that meat out so he could smell it. Now best I can tell, we'll be eatin' our dressing without turkey this year. Put some of that ham left over from breakfast on the table. They get hungry enough, they'll eat it."

Mama had gone into the kitchen in a huff, but that became one of her favorite stories, and Jane knew Bill would hear it today.

In addition to the turkey already roasted, the dressing had been mixed, too, and was in the refrigerator waiting until the last minute to be baked. The butter beans Mama had canned last summer and stored in the light blue Mason jars were poured into a big boiler and seasoned with plenty of bacon drippings. Jimmi peeled potatoes for mashing while Aunt Laura Mae prepared giblet gravy. There were also collards and sweet potatoes to be warmed. Aunt Sami was bringing a Lane cake, and Jimmi had baked pecan pies to add to Mama's fresh coconut cake and ambrosia. By the time Aunt Sami and her crowd arrived, lunch was almost ready.

Uncle Jack blessed the meal, and Jane felt a shudder as she realized how much he sounded like Papa. He was of the same sweet nature as Papa, and she loved him for it.

The conversation was as animated as it had been the night before, but this time Bill entered into it more. He was at ease, and her family was at ease with him. She knew they all approved of him for her; she wondered if he could deal with them and this way of life.

After lunch, the women cleared the table and cleaned the kitchen while the men moaned and groaned about what a wonderful meal it had been and about how they wouldn't be able to eat another bite for a week. As a child, this had been the longest period of time in the year for Jane. No gifts could be unwrapped until the kitchen met Mama's specifications. No dishes left to soak; everything had to be clean and put away. Even now, she found herself hurrying with the last iron skillet, eager to get to the cedar tree Pie and Uncle Jack had cut the week before, now adorned with sweet gum burs and the bubbling lights she had been so in awe of as a child.

She had more money this year and was excited about seeing the reactions of everyone as they opened the gifts she had so painstakingly bought. It was Janese's turn to distribute the bounty, and she was much too slow to suit Jane. Soon, however, the room was aflutter with ribbons, paper, and boxes. Jane had done well. Everybody seemed to love all the things she had spent a year mulling over, selecting, rejecting, and selecting again in an effort to get the perfect present for each person, including engraved sterling silver cuff links for

Bill. She was so pleased and smug that it had not occurred to her that she had received nothing from Bill until he spoke up.

"Jane, did you think I wasn't going to give you anything? I certainly hope I have not done a foolish thing and chosen the wrong time to do this, but here goes. Jane Ellen Robbins, will you marry me?"

With that bombshell announcement and a flourish, he fished a ring box from his jacket pocket and presented it for her to open. She wasn't sure she had the strength. She mustered it quickly, though, and inside found the most gorgeous diamond solitaire she had ever seen. Gasps went round the room as she eased it from its black slot, and he took it and slipped it onto her finger.

"For God's sake, chile, tell the boy somethin' 'fo he faint dead away!" good old reasonable Mama advised.

"Yes! Yes! Yes! Yes! Yes!" was all she could utter as he, shouting with joy, lifted her up and twirled her around the room while her family cheered and applauded.

Because they both had to get back to work quickly, they arose early the day after Christmas for their last day in Alabama. Jane took Bill to Papa's grave and tried to explain the special relationship between her and this first man she had ever loved. Then they walked up to the Wambles house, still boarded up just as it had been before she left. There she tried to make him understand hers and Lynn's relationship but found words inadequate.

After a leisurely lunch of leftovers with all the family, the couple loaded up for the trip back to the airport. The goodbyes were not long, and no tears were shed. Hers was a stoic family, but there was a knot in the pit of Jane's stomach as she looked back from the cattle gap and saw Pie, Jimmi, Aunt Laura Mae, Uncle Jack, and a stooped Mama on Mama's front porch waving when they saw her turn her head back in their direction. She knew she had to go back to New York and was eager to begin her wedding plans, but she would never be comfortable leaving her family.

She and Bill took a short detour by Donny and Sadie's to see them and little Sara and to exchange gifts. The baby was just beginning to toddle and to utter a few words, and the three of them seemed so happy in their tiny apartment. Donny and Sadie approved of Bill, too, although Donny did keep her guessing for a while, as a bit of payback. They oohed and aahed over her ring, and Sadie made Jane promise to keep them abreast of the wedding plans.

The entire plane ride home was devoted to her grilling him on his reaction to her family. After about the tenth or twelfth question, Bill finally attempted to stop her.

"For heaven's sake, Jane, I love you and want to marry you. Do you honestly think I care what your family is like?"

That, for sure, was not the answer she was waiting to hear, and she let him know it.

"Well, Mr. High and Mighty, you don't like them. They're too country and poor for you, is that it? Well, I'll have you know that's how I was raised, and I'm just as country and poor as the rest of them!"

The young man in the turban sitting across the aisle turned and looked at what he must have assumed was a lovers' quarrel, probably unable to understand most, if any, of what she had said.

Not even attempting to conceal his smile, Bill tried to calm the irate Jane he had never seen before. "Settle down! I was teasing you. You have been so uptight you couldn't even relax and enjoy the time at home as you should have. You were so worried about my impression of your family.

"How could I possibly find any fault with your folks? I envy you the warmth and camaraderie. The love that flows among you is amazing. The bantering and sharing that go on around Mama's table is unlike anything I have ever experienced before. My parents love me, but I have never felt they had time for me.

" There was so much Father had to do when I was young to advance his young law practice, and my mother had to excel socially to promote his career. I often didn't fit into the scheme of things. My summers were spent at camp and with my grandparents in the city. My first hero was the cop who patrolled the beat on their street my fourth summer, not my father.

"Because I am the only child of only children, I never had cousins to play with, either. Sally is the closest relative I have near my own age, and we aren't really close. You can't possibly understand what you have in your family."

With tears in her eyes, she squeezed his hand. "I love you, Bill Hammond, and I think I might still marry you, even thought you did try a little hard to snow Mama."

He was apparently taken aback with that accusation. "I did no such thing!" he defended himself. "I just found her so charming and honest and real. Not one ounce of pretense there. As for still wanting to get married, I'm more than a little worried about that temper of yours. I didn't know you had it in you to get that mad."

"I don't get mad often. It takes a lot set me off, but say anything bad about my family, and I'm on you like a duck on a June bug. Remember that, Mr. Hammond," Jane warned.

"I'll certainly try! I don't want to lose use of any of my body parts." Their fellow traveler, the Arab, settled back into his seat as Jane and Bill embraced, rather uncomfortably in the tiny space.

"Speaking of your family," Bill began, "what do you know about the girl Pie is planning to marry?"

Now it was she who was taken aback. "What girl? I haven't heard anything about any of this. How do you know?"

"Well," began a surprised Bill, "he told me after we went to bed Christmas Eve. I just assumed you knew already. She is someone he met in church about a year ago. She moved to the region from Detroit to care for her grandmother who had bone cancer. Seems the older lady died six weeks ago, and Pie was afraid his girl would go back home; so he proposed, and she accepted. They are going to live with Mama. Uncle Jack feels like she is beginning to need some help. Are you sure they hadn't mentioned it in their letters?"

Of course she was sure! She couldn't believe it! Pie had confided in Bill before he had in her. She didn't know whether to feel flattered that he liked her choice in men enough to share such an intimate secret with him or to be hurt and angry that she had heard the news second hand. She chose the former for the moment. But living with Mama? She was surprised when she realized she was jealous. As much as she loved Pie and knew Mama probably did need help, she felt her grandmother was hers. But she couldn't dwell on any of that now. There were too many positive aspects of her life. She was getting married.

The decision to have sex the first time was hers; although, he certainly did not object. And to say it was wonderful would be to diminish its impact. After all those months of arguing with her own body and impulses, the physical fulfillment of the relationship brought a release and relief she couldn't have dreamed of. She didn't have the background to fashion such dreams. She only hoped and prayed Mama would have understood, had she known. She doubted it, but Jane had no regrets. She considered herself emotionally married to Bill already. For as long as they remained together, this night would mark their anniversary date.

Her colleagues at work planned a lingerie shower at Sandra's, and Jane appreciated their generosity and kindness. She realized she had been somewhat aloof, and she felt guilty. She really liked them; she just didn't form close relationships easily. Thank God, again, for Bill and their closeness.

While the thoughts of marrying filled her every waking moment, the wedding itself required little contemplation. Because her family couldn't afford to come up and because Bill's parents were so in involved in their own lives, his grandparents' minister would perform the ceremony at the folks' apartment. Bill's oldest friend and first partner from the force would stand up with him; while Sandra would be her maid of honor and only guest. The evening of Valentine's Day was agreed upon as the appropriate time.

Jane wore a white wool suit, much like the one worn on that first Christmas they were together. She had no veil or bouquet. Both seemed to her a waste of money for such a simple rite. Bill dressed in his gray suit, and the few guests also wore church clothes.

Their wedding trip was a long weekend in the Poconos. A cruise to Mexico, a gift from his parents, would follow in the summer. Upon their return from the mountains, they moved her into Bill's apartment. It was the bigger of the two and in a better section of town.

The search for a house began immediately. Bill insisted on one with a large fenced-in back yard so that he could play with the three boys and three girls he was planning. He would compensate for his own lonely childhood with a big family. While Jane hoped she could reduce the number considerably, she was also eager for children. They used no form of birth control after the wedding.

By the time they left for Cozumel in July, they still hadn't settled on a house, but Jane was six weeks pregnant. The ship's food was delicious, and although she sometimes had to drag Bill to the midnight buffet, she never missed a meal. She was afraid she was going to gain a ton, but he promised to love her even while she was losing it—every ounce.

While snorkeling with a group from the ship, Bill watched over her like a mother hen, protecting her and the baby. She thought it was hilarious when it was he who slipped and hit his knee on the coral. When she saw the pain in his eyes, the event lost its humor. It required the strong backs of a couple of young men they had known only a few days to get him back to the tender returning them to the ship. Once aboard the larger boat, the ship's doctor gave him pain pills, put a splint on the leg, and put him on crutches with explicit instructions to see his own physician when they returned home.

The swelling was really bad when they entered the New York orthopedist's examining room, and a series of X-rays was ordered. Since all movement was obviously excruciatingly painful, the ordeal wore Bill out. However, no breaks were detected, and they were able to leave rather quickly. Jane hurried to get him home and into bed with one of the strong pain relievers. He was sleeping soundly when the phone rang.

"Mrs. Hammond, this is Dr. Wynberg's office," the unfamiliar voice said. "We found a suspicious looking area on your husband's knee. The doctor would like him back in the office tomorrow morning at 8:00 for further tests."

She was paralyzed. What could be so urgent as to warrant a trip back so soon? She went into the bedroom and watched him sleep, fighting back her tears so near the surface. Then she went into the living room to call Donny. When he answered the phone, her tears came. He tried unsuccessfully at first to quiet her. Finally, the voice of reason she had depended on for so long broke through her resistance.

"Jane Ellen, you're jumpin' the gun, sugah." his soft, Southern drawl assured her. "This could be lots of things. I know what you're thinkin', but nothing says it's definitely cancer. Don't get Bill upset. Gently tell him the news when he wakes up, and get him there by 8:00. We'll call our Sunday school class members and start a prayer chain. Do you want me to get in touch with Mama and the others? We could be down there in twenty minutes."

"No," a somewhat calmer Jane agreed. "You're probably right. Maybe it is nothing. No use in worrying until we know for sure. As for the chain, Bill and I both would appreciate the prayers very much."

"I'll be at work tomorrow," Donny continued. "Call me at the station the minute you know something. We love you and are here for you, but try to get a grip now. You don't want to alarm him."

"Thanks, Donny. I love y'all, too. Give the two women in your household a hug for me. I just needed to hear a rational voice, and I knew I could count on you for that, as always," Jane sighed.

It was early afternoon, but Jane crawled in beside her handsome, six-foot-two, robust husband, held him close, and cried gently, so as not to disturb him, but the tears fell profusely. She got up to use the bathroom twice that afternoon and night but otherwise stayed by his side, never sleeping a wink. When he awakened early the next morning, refreshed and in much less pain, they made love gently and watched the sun rise outside their bedroom window.

Somewhere around 6:30 she broke the news just as she had rehearsed it hundreds of times during the long night. She waited for his response. What she got was a full three minutes of silence. She leaned up and looked down on him to see his reaction. When he finally spoke, it was with tears in his eyes and a quiver in his voice.

"Jane, I have known more love since I met you than in all of the twenty-eight years before. If this is a false alarm, as I pray it is, we can laugh about it when we're old and waiting for the grandchildren to come over for milk and cookies. If it's bad news, just know that I would not change one thing in my life. I'm happy, my love. How many people do you know who can truly say that? You have made my life complete. None of us is guaranteed any time. Each day is a gift. You know that. Now, let's get dressed and go get this over with."

She waited in the reception area with a roomful of other anxious people and pretended to read a magazine. When the nurse called her to join Bill in the examining room, she rose and hit the floor in a dead faint.

She was on the doctor's table when she revived, and Bill was seated beside her in a chair that should have been hers. He was gently rubbing her hand as he spoke. "Thank, God, Jane! We thought you were trying to check out on us. What happened? Are you all right?"

Her head hurt terribly, and she could feel the goose egg forming just over her right eye where she obviously first made contact with the floor, but she assured him as best she could. "I'm fine. Just no breakfast, the pregnancy, and this" (indicating with her eyes, the room).

She felt so stupid and weak. She was supposed to be encouraging him, but he was the one offering support and strength. She hated her lack of fortitude and was extremely angry with herself. She had always loathed women who tried to seem weak for their own advantage. She feared at the moment she appeared to be one of those women. No time for analysis now, however.

She sat up and looked at Dr. Wynberg who had been hovering over her for any sign of concussion, which he didn't find. She didn't like his expression.

Accepting the fact that she really was going to be all right, he answered her unvoiced question concerning her husband. "I can not say for sure until we get the results from the lab, but my experience with this sort of thing causes me to be a bit pessimistic. Call me the day after tomorrow, and I should be able to tell you something more definitely. Until then, try to focus on something else. If you're religious, I would suggest prayer."

The newlyweds with their first child on the way went home to spend a day and a half in agonizing limbo. Each tried to present a happy front, but the effort failed miserably. She couldn't put on a happy face and "play the Pollyanna game" as Mama called it. Not this time. While Bill slept, a result of more medicine, she called Donny at work. This time he didn't try to be so optimistic as before and again asked about getting in touch with her relatives; again she nixed it

A long letter from Pie came in the mail that day, detailing his plans to renovate Mama's house, with Uncle Jack's help. They had already connected the old house to the county water system and had bought a water heater. There would be a bath, another bedroom, paint inside and out, and phone lines to both houses in due time. The letter was so upbeat, with even a note from Dot, Pie's new wife. And while Jane had long since gotten over her anger and hurt with Pie for confiding in Bill before he did her, the light air of this missive served only to deepen her own despair.

When the haze of the interim finally passed, they returned to the doctor's office. Bill's strength of resolve had about worn itself out. He entered Dr. Wynberg's chamber dejectedly, squeezing her hand.

"Mr. and Mrs. Hammond, please be seated," the doctor abruptly instructed. Just as abruptly he stated, "I'm afraid the news isn't good. The biopsy shows a number of malignant spots that have, I fear, spread throughout the skeletal system. We can send you to a radiologist for treatments, but I would advise against it. In my opinion, that would diminish the quality of life left and would probably do nothing to improve the survival odds. The disease is too advanced, I believe."

"How long, Doctor?" It was Bill's strong voice. Jane had been numb and incapable of speech since they entered the room.

"A year at most—perhaps much less," a sympathetic Dr. Wynberg replied.

Jane was certain this was some sort of horrible nightmare. Must the men she loved be destined to die and leave her just when she needed them most?

The couple went about their lives as normally as the ever-present uninvited quest allowed them. They discussed names for the baby, planned the nursery, talked about their dream house, and tried to pretend the sickness wasn't there. Toward the end, the excruciating pain Bill experienced made the charade impossible.

Two months after the diagnosis, on a hot, rainy August morning, Bill died in her arms on the bed they had shared since the night when they first made love. That afternoon with his grandparents in the living room, she went into the bathroom and miscarried. Her obstetrician made a house call, unheard of in New York, and tried unsuccessfully to persuade her to spend at least one night in the hospital. Instead, she spent the night alone, never having felt so empty in her life.

She asked for, and was granted, permission from her in-laws to name the child as she and Bill had planned. So William James Hammond, IV, was buried beside his father. She prayed they could play together in a big fenced-in yard in heaven. She prayed there was a heaven. There was some comfort in her belief that with Little Bill there, Bill would not be without family.

His parents and grandparents and her associates from work had rallied around her, but it was the home folks who got her through. Pie and Uncle Jack had sped up the phone installations when they first learned of Bill's diagnosis, and the lines between her apartment and their houses and between her apartment and Donny's stayed busy. Donny and Sadie flew to New York for the funeral services. They hadn't told her they were coming; probably they knew she would have discouraged it for financial reasons, but she had never been so thankful to see anyone. She worried about how they afforded the plane tickets, but she didn't ask. They could stay with her only one night before returning to Montgomery where little Sara was with Sadie's parents, and the two of them had to get back to work and Donny back to school. He was attending college at night.

The day after the funeral, Jane received a sympathy card from Lynn. It contained no personal message and was merely signed "Lynn," but Jane knew how difficult it must have been to accomplish even that. The envelope was postmarked "Selma." The letter couldn't leave the local post office for obvious reasons. Jane guessed that Miss Pat had mailed it for her daughter. She longed for real interaction with the dearest female friend she had ever had but knew Lynn's current circumstances made it impossible.

Alone once more in a city she had never liked, she settled again into a routine of work, sleep, work, sleep. The phone calls to and from home became less and less frequent. Everyone had to get back to his or her life, and she didn't choose to weight them down with her loss.

Chapter IX

Initially, Jane made a point to see Bill's grandparents every weekend. The three often attended church together, and she lunched with them afterward. She loved them dearly, but their presence made his absence all the more pronounced. As the weeks progressed, her visits to the couple became less and less frequent. She felt as if she were abandoning them but also wondered if seeing her also intensified their feelings of loss. She prayed she was being kind with her separation, not merely selfish.

Each month when her period began, she mourned anew the loss of hers and Bill's child. When she saw a mother with a baby or heard a crying infant, she felt an emptiness in her center.

Sleep became her refuge. It was her drug of choice just as alcohol or heroin was to many. She escaped to it and within it. Dreams often brought visions of her husband and baby - sometimes even of Papa and her faceless mother. Sleep was the opiate that consumed the majority of her existence.

She also continued to depend on her spirituality for support. She prayed, read Papa's old Bible, and attended church regularly in a search for solace and explanations. One Sunday morning after worship services, the minister, Brother James, asked her to wait a few minutes after all the other parishioners had gone.

"Jane," the kindly minister began, "I have watched as you have gone from a vibrant, happy woman to a thin, shell of a being who exhibits no semblance of living. There are many things in your life you can't change—unpleasant, awful things. But, there are also things you do control. Grab hold of those things and make them as good as they can be. Only you and God know what those things are."

She was surprised at his observation of her. "Brother James, I have nothing that brings me the least joy. Even religion and God are beginning to seem hollow. I come to church, I read the Bible, and I pray, but nothing changes. I wonder if I have offended God somehow. There has been hate and distrust in my life, but I've tried to put that behind me. I admit, I still hold on to some of it. I keep at religion, though, because I do believe God works on His time frame, not on that of us mortals."

The minister countered, "I think you're being too hard on yourself. You're not being punished by God. All of us have sins in our lives and weaknesses we have to fight daily. The relief of some of your oppressive pain will come for you in due time. In the meantime, you've got to take better care of yourself. What about your job and your friends? Don't they bring you any joy?"

"Bill was my only close friend here. I don't make friends easily," she admitted. "As far as my job is concerned, it is the only one I have ever known except for cleaning houses with Mama, back home, and my cafeteria work in college. It pays the bills and allows me a sense of financial security, but I hate it, loathe it, despise it!"

She was shocked at the words spewing forth from her own mouth. She had never known she had any feelings whatever about her job. She didn't know she was allowed to. Jobs were not meant to evoke feelings—they were just what you had to do. They weren't to be liked or disliked. Nobody in her family had ever discussed, to her knowledge, liking or disliking what they did for a living. They had the jobs they could get.

"Jane, you must find work you can enjoy," her very perceptive minister advised. "You can't continue in such a depressed state about your personal life and spend each work day miserable. There has to be some peace and contentment somewhere, or you're going to die, physically and emotionally."

His last statement frightened her, but she had a feeling he was right. "Tell me what do, Brother James. I have trained to do nothing else."

"That decision is yours, child, but I believe God can help you to make it. The two of you must figure out your needs and abilities. I know only that He intends for you to be happy, but *you* must take the necessary steps. I'm here if you need me," the man of God promised, "and I'll continue praying for you."

"Thank you, Brother James," Jane said. "You've certainly given me much food for thought."

The next Friday, after much prayer and thought, Jane gave her two weeks' notice and applied for a job on the police force. She realized it was what she had to do. The chief, Bill's old boss and friend, gave her a really hard time. She understood that he questioned her motives, but her persistence wore him down. She was unemployed only a week before she reported for duty as a cop on the beat in a neighborhood in Harlem much like her first community in the city.

From the beginning, she knew she had made the right decision. This was what she was destined to do, she believed. Her feet ached and her back was stiff as she sank into a hot tub that first night, but she felt a contentment she hadn't known since before Bill's diagnosis, and although she dreamed about her love, she awoke before dawn the following morning eager for the day's work. She had a long, slow cup of coffee and relished her new purpose for being.

Each shift brought further insights into her new profession, and she was as eager to learn this as she had been to learn her texts earlier. She never missed an opportunity to attend a professional seminar or to take a continuing education course.

She applied for the police academy and was quickly accepted. As a college educated black woman in the early '70s,

Affirmative Action was definitely to her advantage. She believed in her own abilities enough to think she would have gotten there eventually, but she was grateful to the Civil Rights Movement for having insured the speed. Naturally, given her proclivity for learning, once again she graduated at the top of her class.

She worked in a variety of positions before her assignment to public relations, swiftly advancing to its head. It was her pleasure to defend, to the citizenry, the force she believed in so strongly and loved so dearly. She also enjoyed tremendously the opportunities her job afforded her to meet the city's youth in an effort to encourage them and to act as a buffer between them and the law.

Children were such a blessing—even the ones who sometimes took the wrong path. In her first profession, she had often lost patience with delinquent adults, but delinquent children and teens touched her heart and evoked her best. She gave her job her all and felt so fulfilled in that aspect of her life.

Her social life was a different matter. Church was the only real contact she had with anyone outside her job. She continued to see Bill's family occasionally and socialized with her fellow officers when police business necessitated it, but nothing was really gratifying. She deliberately kept everyone at arm's length as a means to prevent painful separation.

She bought a small house with a yard (more for Bill than for her herself) and got her first mongrel at the pound. She rationalized that it was for protection, but given the animal's timid nature, she knew it was primarily for companionship. That and the satisfaction she derived from being needed, if only by a dog. Days he spent in the fenced-in yard and doghouse, but nights he spent inside with her, sharing her house and her affection.

For twenty years that was her life. Not much changed during that time except the dog. She went back home when she could and even convinced Mama to travel up to see her once a year after Bill's death. Not on a plane, though, for goodness sake! Mama wasn't getting up in the air for anybody, not even her Jane Ellen. She caught a ride with a family who visited relatives in Virginia each year, and Jane met her there. She stayed a week, never more. Although Jane looked forward to the visits, and although she needed her grandmother so much, she never insisted that they extend the stay. The old lady was clearly miserable in the urban setting. So, each time, when the day arrived to drive her back to Virginia, Jane sadly made the drive.

The dog who served as her daily companion changed as one died and was replaced quickly by an equally worthless mutt, and Jane mourned each of them as she buried him or her in the back yard in a ceremony attended by her alone. This was as close as she chose to come to a relationship.

The faces of the people she dealt with at work changed, too, and toward the end of her career, the severity of the crimes increased dramatically as the ages of the perpetrators decreased, also dramatically. The children she loved so deeply and tried so desperately to save were more and more often becoming both the victim and the victimizer. Murders, robberies, even rapes were being committed by what she considered babies.

As hard as she worked, the frustration of her job was beginning to outweigh the satisfaction. She knew it was time to give it up when a seven-year-old boy shot and killed his five-year-old neighbor over the last grape lollipop. So, when she completed her tenure and could retire, she did.

She said the few goodbyes needed—Sandra and her family, the others from her old welfare office who were still around, and Bill's parents. His grandparents had died within six months of each other a little over eight years earlier. She had not been able to admit it at the time, but there was a sense of relief at their deaths. She no longer had to feel guilty about not contacting them often or depressed about seeing them without Bill.

Her Sunday school class gave her a going away party and made her promise to keep in touch, but she was not really close to any of them and never saw them outside church activities. She knew she would probably never see any of them again, and that was all right. Brother James had died, too, and while she liked the new young minister, he wasn't as compassionate as his predecessor. Thankfully, before his death, Brother James had seen the fruition of his advice in her life.

The house sold rather quickly, and preparations for her exodus were reasonably simple. The crates were packed and waiting for the movers. One suitcase was readied for the trip, and the latest dog, Abner's, food was loaded into the trunk. It was actually depressing to think that she had spent most of her adult life here, yet leaving was so easy.

She wished for Mama now, as she often did, but especially when there were changes in her life. She particularly would have liked to share homecoming with her, but her grandmother's long bout with diabetes had finally ended two years earlier, and Mama had died at home with family surrounding her. Jane had made it just two days before the end. The doctors had told Uncle Jack death was near and to call everyone in. All the children and grandchildren except Jane's daddy and Jimmi were in the house with the old woman when she passed into the next world. Jimmi had made her own passage after a heart attack two years prior. Her husband was rearing their two teenaged daughters alone, and doing an exceptional job, according to Pie. Jane had gone home for Jimmi's funeral but not for Uncle Bud's. He had died of tetanus after stepping on a rusty nail eight months ago. Thoughts of those family members who would not be home to greet her paraded through Jane's mind as she readied the old sedan for the long drive.

On her way out of New York, she took a side trip by the cemetery to say goodbye to Bill and the baby. The morning was foggy and cool, and Abner was not at all comfortable being there; so she had cut the visit short. Besides, what was there to say? While her mind assured her that she was not abandoning her husband and baby, her heartache was akin to that she had felt at their deaths. But she knew Bill's chief aim in life after their meeting had been to make her happy, and she believed her happiness lay in Alabama. She felt her sanity depended upon her reconnection to the human race. She had led an isolationist existence long enough.

She didn't know what her place would be in the New South, or even if she would have one. She knew she had to find out. She had left home for financial independence and had achieved that goal. She was not wealthy by any means, but Bill's insurance money, her savings, and the profit from the sale of the house, coupled with her monthly retirement check were enough to insure her never having to work again, if that's what she chose. New York had been good to her in that respect. She was tired, though, of the grime, the cold, the crime, the breakneck speed of daily life, and the impersonal attitude.

When she phoned Pie to tell him of her decision to retire and come home, she told him, "I want to see someone I love and who loves me on a regular basis. I don't want to go out my door without encountering at least one person who knows me by name and whom I know the same way. I don't want to shovel snow another time, and I want honest-to-goodness fried chicken and turnips and collards with grease floating on top."

"Sounds to me like you are definitely homesick. Nothin' to cure that but to get in that piece of crap you call a car and drive as far south as it'll take you. We'll meet you and bring you the rest of the way when it puts you down side the road," a chuckling Pie assured her.

Chapter X

Pie, Uncle Jack, and Donny had each offered her a place to stay until she could decide on permanent living arrangements, but she had rented a house in Montgomery through an agency. She had been independent far too long to share anybody else's space. Besides, Abner didn't need a bunch of strangers trying to tell him what to do. Except for his relationship with her, he had been a loner, too.

He was an excellent traveling companion. She had bent his ear for miles with her chatter about the wonders of the South, and he appeared to listen at least a part of the way, but he slept throughout much of the monologue, too. No matter—he was company.

It was 3:40 A.M. when she pulled into the driveway of her new home. She had received photos of it inside and out from the agent, and in her headlights it looked just as she had thought, in what appeared to be a neat neighborhood. Right now, it didn't matter; sleep was the only important thing. It could have been her old room at the Y, and it would have looked good at that point.

The movers had made it ahead of her, and crates were everywhere. She slipped out of her bra, initially reviewed the house, used the bathroom, turned on the air conditioning and hit the sofa with Abner at her feet. When she awoke nine hours later, Abner was whining and scratching on the den door. She let him out into the big, fenced in back yard and saw for the first time her surroundings in the light of day. She was pleased. Nothing fancy, but suitable. She showered, dressed, and took Abner to meet the family.

She allowed herself the luxury of settling in slowly. A relaxed pace was something she had never previously experienced. Crates were opened one or two at a time. Often, days would go by without any work, just visiting and soaking up the emotional and physical warmth of her surroundings.

As soon as her bedroom was arranged, she placed her three most prized possessions—a tattered old Bible, a yellowed sheet of wrapping tissue used as a book mark at Daniel III, and a picture of her and Bill on their wedding day—on the table beside her bed.

The first time back in the old house was a strange experience. Pie and Dot had invited all the family for supper to celebrate Jane's homecoming. They had done fabulous things with the place. White vinyl siding covered the old tongue-in-groove boards that Papa had hammered into place himself so many years earlier. The newspaper had been stripped off all the interior walls and replaced with dry wall, painted an off white throughout the house. Insulation made the rooms much more comfortable, and an air conditioner unit in the big bedroom and one in the living room assured a level of cool air Jane had not believed possible.

Mama's old enamel kitchenware containers with their nicks and holes that had held the flowers in the yard and on the front porch had been replaced with store-bought clay pots, but the same colors and varieties of inexpensive plants Jane remembered from her childhood still held their place—pink petunias, orange and yellow zinnias and marigolds, red geraniums, and pink and red begonias. On either side of the front steps still stood Mama's blue hydrangeas—the same ones Jane had watered so many times with Mama's old blue speckled pitcher with the patched bottom. Trellises holding the morning glory vines were gone from the front yard, but the white rose bush still climbed on the back fence just outside the kitchen door. Jane remembered the time the crazy rooster Mama was fattening as Sunday dinner for the preacher had chased a barefoot Jane Ellen around the yard and through that rose bush. For a week she had picked the painful thorns out of her arms and feet.

The yard was never swept now. It had to be mowed regularly because Bermuda grass intermingled with bahia that shot up a foot overnight grew in every corner.

The back walnut tree that had once supported a tire swing of her youth had been cut down and cleared away after lightning struck it, creating a danger to the house. Uncle Jack had had it cut and planed at the sawmill, and its beautiful grained wood now graced the walls of Pie and Dot's room. The plum bush and the peach tree, the one that never bore edible fruit in her recollection but produced lovely profuse blooms and the keenest switches in the world, were also noticeably absent from the yard.

The place was neat and clean, inside and out, and Dot had done a very good job decorating it, but it wasn't home any more, and Jane was saddened by that fact. That Mama's rocker still sat by the fireplace and that Papa's straight chair with its cowhide bottom still held its place in the kitchen comforted her. It was in that straight chair with its tan and white seat still hanging on to a small portion of its original owner's hair that a nappy haired little girl had spent many happy hours in an old man's lap listening to stories read and remembrances related.

Along with all the other changes, the smells were also different. When Jane realized that, she also understood for the first time that most of her lasting impressions of her childhood were of smell. Lynn's house had smelled clean and open. Hers had smelled of smoke from the fireplace and the Cashmere Bouquet soap Mama had always bought because it was mild, yet cheap. She also remembered the metallic smell of the water dipper that brought cool liquid from a bucket pulled up from the well that smelled of earth. There had been the marshy scent of the cow pen, and the stuffy, acrid stench of the outhouse, or "toilet," as they had always called it.

The good smells were gone, too. The wood stove had been replaced by an electric range, and no ham frying in the iron skillet met her olfactory nerves in the kitchen. No Old Spice or Evening in Paris lingered in what had been Mama and Papa's room.

Lemon-scented potpourri on the bathroom vanity was pleasant, and cinnamon greeted her in the kitchen. Lemon oil scented the air conditioning unit in the den. While all were nice, they didn't smell like her recollections of the house, and Jane felt a pang of homesickness and nostalgia that nothing less than middle age could bring.

The icebox in the kitchen, with its ever-overflowing drip pan had given up its position to a side-by-side refrigerator. Modern plumbing in the kitchen and bath and generous lighting throughout the house brightened what once had been a dark abode.

The outdoor toilet was gone, and a compost pile appropriately stood in its old home site. The cow pen had also disappeared. The fence between it and the garden had been removed increasing the size of the garden plot. Tomatoes, butter beans, crowder and black-eyed peas, okra, squash, and cucumbers still grew in abundance in the soil made richer by the natural fertilizer left behind by all the Bessies who had given their milk and sometimes their all to provide for the Robbins family.

The sofa Papa had bought just before his death still sat in the front room. The plastic covering was gone, and the original beige fabric had long ago worn out and been replaced the latest time by a soft pink floral.

The smokehouse was still standing, but no hams or sausages hung on the wire extended from its ceiling rafters. Aunt Laura Mae and Dot now used the building as storage space for some of the hundreds of jars of canned fruits and vegetables they put up each year. The fig tree still grew at the northeast corner. Jane made a trip through the smokehouse with Pie as a part of her tour on the grounds on her first visit after moving back.

The air was much cooler inside it than outside, and the pungent odor of long-ago lard spilled on the boards of the shelves and on the ground mingling with that of the dirt itself evoked memories of carefree days of play with the rest of the children while the grownups performed the backbreaking, tedious work of killing hogs. The smells also evoked recollections of the delicious salty pork that could never be replicated no matter how expensive the cut in the market. And she remembered the tenderloin. That precious tiny strip of fresh pork that was always eaten with biscuits and gravy the night of hog killing and no other time!

Mama's old wash shed still stood at the north end of the smokehouse. The shelves that had supported the scrub tubs at Mama's waist level were intact. Jane tried to recall the smell of the harsh lye soap Mama made and used to scrub the work clothes clean, but she couldn't quite nail that scent down. She did recollect that she and mama had spent many hours here — just the two of them while Mama washed and she entertained herself.

The two reunited cousins walked to the south end of the building where the butchered swine had hung from the rafters to be bled, cleaned, and processed. They sat on the sturdy shelf that once held utensils of the butchering and reminisced.

She began, "Pie, remember how we used to beg to stir the fat and how Mama and Papa kept the peach tree switch for the express purpose of swatting us away from the pot. Papa said neither one of us had sense enough to stay out of the fire."

"Yeah," Pie joined in, "and I also remember the time you fell backwards into the vat of chittlins and begged Jimmi not to tell me you fell in the 'gutlins.'" Just like I couldn't smell you a mile off. Mama stripped you to the bone and threw your clothes on the fire. You must have been all of three. I called you 'gutlin' for a long time till you dropped the flat iron on my toe and broke it because I called you that in front of company."

"I don't think I dropped that iron on you," an innocent Jane continued. "The way I recall, it just fell off the mantle as you walked by. I do remember the 'gutlin' thing. I was so afraid you would call me that after I started school. I had enough trouble with Miss Cain without giving her any more ammunition."

"The funniest thing I remember about our childhood was the time the wharf rat ran up Mama's dress when she and Aunt Sammie were shucking corn in the crib. Me and you and Jimmi was runnin' around outside chasin' Papa's old coon dog; the one with the notched ear. I can't remember that mutt's name."

"Trouble. Don't you remember, Mama got so mad when Papa brought it home. Said it would be nothing but more trouble for her to take care of."

"That's right." Pie recalled. "It turned out to be Mama's shadow, and I don't remember Papa ever huntin' with it. Anyway, we was playin' with that dog when Mama let out a blood curdlin' scream. The dog started barkin' at the top of his lungs, and the three of us flew in to see 'bout Mama. When we got inside, she and Aunt Sammie were sittin' on a stack of corn, and Mama was holding on to something in the skirt of her dress. About that time, she screamed, turned her dress loose and jumped up. Aunt Sammie was tryin' to help, but Mama wouldn't sit still long enough and couldn't tell her what was wrong. Mama grabbed at the thing again and held it until it squirmed and tried to bite her, and then she had to let it loose a second time. She tore that dress skirt to shreds before that pore rat finally got out or before any of the rest of us knew what was wrong with her. Even Aunt Sammie hadn't known all the time she was tryin' to help. I thought Mama was havin' a fit"

"Oh, Lord, I can still see us making a circle around Mama to get her home before anybody else could see her in her disarray. She was so proud. I know what dress it was. It had a pink bodice and a pink floral skirt. She made it out of feed sacks. I had one similar to it she made from flour sacks on that old foot-pedal machine she had that we used to love to push when we didn't think she was looking," Jane reminisced.

"Do you remember how Mama and Papa always argued over how much seasoning to put in the sausage until the year Mama got mad, let him do it his way, and they had to throw all of 'em out because they were too hot even for him to eat?"

"Sure do," Pie assured her, "but I can't believe you do. You were so young when that happened. How could you possibly remember?"

"Pie, I've spent a lifetime piecing together bits and pieces, trying with all my might to recall any and everything possible. I worshipped him, you know."

"I know, Jane Ellen. I was jealous of your relationship with him and Mama. Daddy tried to explain that they were the only parents you had, but they was my grandparents, too, and I thought they loved you more."

A surprised Jane replied, "I never thought of that. I certainly never meant to hurt you or any of the other grandchildren. I just loved them so much; I didn't realize I was being selfish."

"Of course you didn't," Pie assured her. That's one reason I had such a tough time dealin' with it. You was so sweet and innocent, and I loved you like a sister, but I was jealous all the same. When Mama told me Papa had wanted me to have the house, I was shocked. I figured it would be yours. And then when you was so free with your blessings on us movin' in, all the bad feelins ended for me. I'm really ashamed to admit all of this to you, even now."

Now it was her turn to reassure. "You shouldn't be, Pie. You were the only male grandchild. I thought that's how it was supposed to be, and you and Dot took such good care of Mama. It was so nice to know she could stay home with people she loved until the last. You know how miserable she would have been and how miserable she would have made everybody else in a nursing home. I loved her, but she was a hard-headed soul."

"You got that right, Jane Ellen. She mellowed some, though. I think Dot's easy manner had a lot to do with that. She did send Janese and Denise and them two brats of theirs a'packin' a couple of times. You know she nor Papa never liked them two girls. I guess it was because they was Uncle Bud's."

"That and the fact they were so stupid," Jane added. "I remember, too, how upset Mama got when Denise got pregnant so young, and then Janese came up pregnant six weeks or so later. It was like she thought she had to keep up or something. You know how Mama felt about such things. She said Papa set such store in families living under the same roof, and not a father in sight for those two babies. I don't think Mama ever got over that, and she didn't think Aunt Sami raised enough hell about it."

"You're right. She said Aunt Sami took on the morals of Uncle Bud's crowd instead of raising Bud to our standards," Pie contributed. "Mama always did feel like we was all better than Uncle Bud, and you and me and Jimmi thought we was better than the twins. We was probably mean to 'em. I think about some of the things we did to leave them out of things, and it worries me."

"We thought we were better, all right, but I don't think we tried to exclude them," Jane defended. "They just didn't have much in common with us. You know—things like brains."

"Jane Ellen, you won't do," Pie chuckled. "I worry about Aunt Sami sometimes, but Daddy says she's as well off as she wants to be. She could work some if she would. She's just content to live on Uncle Bud's Social Security from his job at the meat packing plant and the welfare checks them heathen youngus bring in. None of us see them until they need me or Daddy to do somethin' for 'em."

Jane thought for a moment before making her own confession. "Pie, I was happy when you and Dot moved into the house with Mama, but only after Bill had calmed me down and gotten me to see how you being here was best for everybody. At first I was jealous of you having Mama to yourself. I know now I was wrong, and I'm sorry."

"Jane Ellen, you don't have anything to feel guilty about," Pie assured her. "You certainly never let on you was upset. We all just thought you would never come back home. I wadn't tryin' to take anything from you."

"I know that, Pie. That's why I had to confess," Jane said. "Have you been happy? You made the decision to stay here with family and be responsible for the whole tribe. I chose the selfish road and left to take care of myself."

"I never thought of it like that," Pie mused. "I stayed because I wanted to, not because I felt responsible. Of course there was times when I wondered if I did the right thing, and there was even times when I was jealous of you and your big salary, but I wouldn't change a thing. I've give my children a clear understanding of their roots, and I been able to appreciate mine. With Dot workin' part-time as an LPN after she got her license and my job driving the truck the last ten years, we've been all right. Part of the time when the chillun was little, it was tough, but we've always made it. I'm thankful for my lifestyle. Yes, I'm happy. Are you?"

"After Bill died, I thought I could never be happy again. My short time with him was too joyous to express. But when I found a profession I truly enjoyed, little by little I began to enjoy life again. I'm so thankful I had the opportunity to do what I did and so delighted to be finished with it and out of that rat race. And, oh so glad to be home. I've missed it every day since I left. Yes, I guess I'm happy, too," Jane decided.

"Did you ever consider remarryin'?" Pie finally mustered the courage to ask. "You never mentioned anyone in your letters or on the phone, and I didn't know how to ask."

"I guess I chose not to think about it," Jane answered. "Oh, I had people at church and on the force who tried to fix me up with a nephew or the son of a friend or a chum from high school, and I went so far as to have dinner with a few, but nothing serious. I've always had a hard time opening myself up to anyone; you know that. Bill got through my guard somehow. I never let anyone else. Perhaps, someday. I'm not dead yet."

"He's gonna have to be a strong-willed man to deal with you," Pie teased.

"You got that right, Cuz!" Jane shouted as she swatted him gently on the arm.

They had walked over every inch of the home place reminiscing. Dot and the children had gone to town for a few groceries and had left the two of them alone, probably intentionally; Pie's wife was a dear person. This was perhaps the longest uninterrupted time the two of them had ever spent as adults, and they basked in it.

When Dot returned, the two women prepared a huge meal, and the entire family once again gathered around the old table. The family was quite a large one, too. In addition to the boy of Denise and the girl of Janese, Pie and Dot had two girls, seventeen and fourteen. Jimmi's children also joined them, along with their father.

The talk was nonstop, as was the food. It definitely was not Mama's cooking, however. Dot's nursing training had found its way into her kitchen where she prepared healthy things for her family. Jane appreciated her taking such good care of these men so prone to heart disease and diabetes, but the taste of some pork drippings in some of the vegetables and a really rich dessert would have been mighty good, especially with her feet once again under Mama's old table.

Chapter XI

There were many obvious changes affecting her homeland in addition to that of Mama and Papa's place. Miss Cain's schoolhouse was empty and apparently had been for some time. Windowpanes were broken and falling out or missing altogether, the roof had a gaping hole, and the two-seater she had loathed had collapsed into itself. Full integration had come during her college years, and all small local schools in the county had been consolidated into three large ones. The great experiment had never really taken place here except on paper, however. Ninety plus percent of the white parents withdrew their children from the public educational system and enrolled them in the two private schools opened expressly to maintain segregation. Whether the plan had worked or not, Jane was thankful that the move had forced Miss Cain to retire and therefore do no further damage. As a cathartic move, Jane picked up the biggest stick she could find and threw it into a window that still held enough glass to shatter when the wood found its mark.

The landscape was different, too. Gone were large herds of cattle on the great expanses of land. Instead, much of the acreage lay idle, either through government subsidy programs or as hunting preserves. The big Wambles house of her childhood now belonged to a group of wealthy hunters from Connecticut who used it a total of thirty-five to forty days a year as a place to sleep and eat during dove, quail, or deer hunts. The new owners had contracted to have it clean and maintained at all times so they could fly down on a whim when they chose. Jane did not know when or if she would have the heart or the courage to walk up the path to see it. Pie had kept her abreast of it over the year.

Also visibly absent were the estate houses of the landed elite. Oh, the edifices themselves stood and were, for the most part, in excellent state of repair, but the Cadillacs, Lincolns, and Chryslers were gone from the driveways, along with their previous owners. The luxury vehicles were replaced by customized vans, special-order pick-ups, and assorted off-road vehicles belonging to the Yuppies who now lived here and commuted twenty or thirty miles to work each day. Swing sets, sliding boards, and see-saws occupied spaces where wash sheds manned by cheap black labor had sat during her youth.

The biggest change she observed was in the people themselves. There were no longer white jobs and black jobs. Even the local government had a majority black composition. Jane's first experience with this difference came when she went to the probate judge's office for an Alabama driver's license. Every face she saw, including that of the judge himself, was black. She wondered if Mama had fully accepted all this. She figured the word "uppity" had been uttered several times before her grandmother's death.

There was a noticeable change in attitude, too. The races intermingled on the sidewalks, commuted to work together, shared social moments during the workday, and even ate together without self-consciousness or fear. She saw little, if any, visiting in each other's homes and absolutely no mixing of religious activities. Jane laughed to herself when she remembered how upset Mama had been with her about her ride to Montgomery with Donny in his old Volkswagen. She also remembered, with disbelief even now, the young man her own age who at sixteen had been gunned down in his front yard because he, a black, had had the audacity to speak openly to a white girl a year younger when they had met on the concourse in front of the courthouse. It was common knowledge that the "offended" girl's uncle, a local politician, had killed the teen but was never even arrested.

The cultural adjustment from North to South and from the Old South to the New South required some real getting used to. Gradually, however, Jane came to accept what they (whoever they were) had done to her birthplace.

For two years after coming home, she did what she wanted when she wanted with whom she wanted, and it was exactly the lifestyle she needed. Then the boredom began to set in. She had never stood still very long in her life. She found she still needed a prearranged purpose for rising each day. Donny, now a deputy sheriff in the county, had been pressuring her since she arrived to go to work with him. Landes County needed a new "man," and with her background, she would be perfect for the job. Donny, like Jane had made a career of it. And just as she had, he loved it.

After graduating college, he had chosen to remain in the field even though he had excelled academically and had had several lucrative offers outside law enforcement. From the Montgomery Police Department, where he had risen to the rank of assistant chief, he had retired to the quieter, cleaner countryside he also loved as much as she did. The less stressful position of deputy in the small county also allowed him more time for his studies. He had begun working on his law degree before retirement. Going at night, it had taken quite some time, but he was near graduation and the bar exam. Studying was mandatory. After not a little arm-twisting on his part, she accepted the job; the sheriff convinced her that a woman on the force, the county's first, could do a lot for the youth. She began looking for a place for her and Abner in the country.

Rental property was not easy to find—at least not what she needed. There were substandard houses and ancient mobile homes, "trailer houses" to the locals. There was a pillared mausoleum in much need of paint and elbow grease for sale, but she didn't need a fixer-upper at her age, and small was definitely better for just the two of them. She couldn't believe her good fortune when she found the cottage.

It had once been the guesthouse of the wealthy landowner who had lived, with his family, in the much larger house less than a hundred yards up the path. It was a three-bedroom antebellum affair with glistening hardwood floors and beautiful wood molding throughout. A roomy kitchen boasting an oversized pantry and an eating nook had been modernized with electrical appliances but with utmost care to retain its antique ambiance.

A bath had been fashioned in the former study, complete with a claw-footed tub and a pedestal sink. Multi-faceted, multi-colored Tiffany light fixtures; airy white lace curtains; and hooked rugs fashioned from rags added to the charm of an intrinsically adorable house.

Both the cottage and its motherhouse were immaculately landscaped and surrounded by century-old oaks. Jane remembered the place from her childhood and wondered what had happened to the couple whose family had owned it since before the oaks were planted. The young family, including two small children, who had bought it three years earlier now occupied the big house. They were happy to have her as a tenant when they heard her background and judged her to be honest.

She really thought it had been Abner who convinced them. He was on his best behavior the day she viewed the place and completely charmed both Ted and Myra Smith and their children Beth and Jason. The dog would have the run of the entire yard, and the yard was huge. Jane thought Ted was joking when he told her the low rent. She had forgotten the enormous difference between the cost of housing here and in town. This was going to be all right.

She tackled the job of settling in much more purposefully this time. She had had her rest and was refreshed and eager to get started in yet another phase of her life. She was excited, but she was also scared. All her work would now be evident to people whose opinions mattered a lot to her.

She worked closely with Donny, learning the ropes and the idiosyncrasies of most of the citizens. Donny knew everybody by name and the background of each one they met. Who lived where and with whom, and how each made a living -both honestly and dishonestly. He also knew about the graft and corruption in the department and in the county government in general. He was appalled by it and complained often and loudly to her, but only to her. He loved his job and needed it to pay his law school expenses. He just didn't care much for injustice.

Jane loved being back at work. She hadn't realized how much she had missed it, but it didn't take her long to see what Donny meant. There were bootleggers that never got caught hauling sugar to stills within spitting distance of other such operations busted on a regular basis. Gambling houses operated within sight of major highways. Prostitution ran rampant in every corner of the county. Drug dealers made connections and sales even while sheriff department cars cruised by. Beer joints sold to minors and on Sundays, a major no-no in Alabama.

Jane tried to arrest a couple of young blacks selling drugs within fifty yards of a local school; Donny stopped her. "Sorry, Jane, you don't need to do that. Those boys belong to the sheriff, bought and paid for. Just part of the long list of untouchables around here."

"Well, what are we supposed to do? What exactly is our job if not to stop this sort of thing?" a confused, frustrated Jane demanded.

"Jane, we are to ride around and be seen," Donny explained. "Arrest a cow thief or a hog thief every now and then, and don't rock the boat. Pretty much stinks to hell, doesn't it? But that's the way it is."

"I can't do it; won't do it!" an angry Jane stormed. "I've got to do my job or let somebody else have it."

With that, she stormed from the county car she was driving and with a great deal of fortitude and very little forethought, she, with Donny's able-bodied assistance, hauled in the sheriff's protected dealers and made a name for herself. Of course, the punks were out again in a matter of hours, and she and Donny received quite an unpleasant speech, replete with a number of Southern adjectives and nouns from the man who signed their pay checks, but the news of the idiotic, or brave, black woman's spunk spread quickly throughout the small rural area.

There were those to whom she became an instant heroine, but there were those to whom she became an instant threat. To the "old boy" network, she was threatening on several fronts. A woman could not be allowed to make them look bad. And a black woman! She might upset the apple carts of a number of people who were getting quite rich off illegal activities. And there were quite a few blacks in high places who were also benefiting from the trickling down of some of that money; those individuals weren't exactly climbing on her bandwagon, either. Then there were those who didn't think a woman, perhaps especially a black woman, had any business in her job in the first place. This last group was not solely white. The old standbys "uppity" and "biggity" were uttered repeatedly, and her sexual leanings were even questioned in some quarters. The fact that she still spoke with something of a New York brogue didn't do much to advance her cause, either. There were many who still believed "damn Yankee" was one word.

Jane heard much of what was said behind her back, including what was meant for her to hear when she walked by a group gathered or when she entered into a place of business while in uniform. This was not new to her. She had experienced much of the same attitude in New York, and then as now she was amazed that these people apparently did not want anything to change.

While the arrest of the drug dealers caused the sheriff to want her dead, he couldn't fire her. There was no legitimate reason. The legal evidence was too strong in her favor. The tension at the office was so thick, it could be cut. The other deputies were as split in their beliefs as were the general populace, but those who felt she was right kept their beliefs to themselves. The sheriff made no attempt to hide his contempt. So, it was that every day, Jane began her shift in a hostile work environment but determined to do the job as she knew it should be done.

It was Donny who first broached the subject of her running for office. She accused him of having lost his mind and gave a dozen reasons why she couldn't or wouldn't. He didn't dignify her oppositions with a comment but proceeded to declare a litany of reasons why she should at least consider it. When the sheriff changed their shifts so that she and Donny never worked together and threatened his job if their friendship continued, her fate was sealed.

She resigned as deputy immediately and began the worst experience of her professional life. She was no politician; that was evident from the beginning. But she believed in her cause and solicited the help of others who also believed.

Race was an issue; it always was, but she had not emphasized it. Some of her supporters were able orators and civil rights activists who stirred the emotions of as many people as they could reach and played the race card. She was idealistic and hoped someday skin color wouldn't matter, but that day hadn't dawned yet. So, she listened to her advisors and presented herself as African American, a term she loathed. She was black; she liked that term. It was simple, to the point, and she still felt black was beautiful.

Her supporters also included whites who still believed fairness and clean government were important and who supported her financially, emotionally, and politically, if not openly.

Her only opponent, the incumbent, had to win. His lifestyle, pride, manhood, and racial superiority depended on it. The money and liquor flowed freely from his camp, and a number of new automobiles changed hands during the process. Jane's campaign was as ethical as she could make it. She worried about the activities of some of her more vocal supporters who were using her to advance a bigger cause, but she, Pie, and Donny (who resigned a week after she did and took a job as a stock clerk at a supermarket in Montgomery), could be in only so many places at once. She emphasized to all her campaign workers and supporters that a clean sheriff's department was what they were after, beginning with the campaign itself.

Every wire service, news magazine, and broadcast media had interviewed her at least once, and hers had been a fishbowl existence from the moment she had announced her candidacy in March. Not that she really minded; she certainly had nothing to hide. But she hadn't intended to cause such a stir; she just wanted to do the work she loved best surrounded by people she loved most in the place she believed to be the greatest.

The contrast between her and the incumbent, a sixty-four-year-old white male who could trace his lineage directly to Jefferson Davis, had not gone unnoticed by those with notebooks and pens or television cameras and microphones who had come calling during the long, grueling campaign.

She, Donny, and Sadie, and every member of her family were threatened repeatedly. She had to establish a code known only to those in the smallest of her inner circle whereby she could answer the phone. The window in her living room was broken by a flying brick, her car tires were all slashed, a dead black cat was placed on her front steps with a rather graphic note around its neck, and racial slurs were scrawled on Ted and Myra's side porch. Jane offered to move, but they insisted she stay, and they became quite actively involved in her campaign—stuffing envelopes, calling their friends, and even knocking on doors. Abner was sent to stay with Uncle Jack and Aunt Laura Mae, solely for his protection, since at least one or both of them would be at home with him at all times.

By the time the last doorbell had been rung, the last placard nailed to a post, the last barking dog appeased, the last sagging porch crossed, the last bigot fended off, and the last interview granted, she was totally drained and totally pessimistic.

She voted early, flashed her best smile for the television cameras, and spent the rest of the day at Pie's, taking a long nap in Mama and Papa's old bed, with Abner at her feet. At six that evening, when the polls closed and the results started coming in, Dot roused her from her dreams, and the entire family rode to Parksville to deal with the news. Donny was already there when she arrived, as were Ted and Myra.

For three long hours they talked in whispers as the boxes were counted, the results posted, and the race volleyed back and forth between the two candidates. Neither ever commanded a large lead. At 9:15, all boxes and the absentee votes were in, and she had won by eighty-seven votes—the smallest margin of victory in the county's recorded history, even though the population was seventy-five percent black. She was female. That made her part of a more denigrated minority than her color ever could. Many of her people couldn't pull the lever for a woman, even one of their own. "Her people," "their own," more terms she loathed. All the people here were her people. She had grown up with them. Besides that, she probably had white relatives among the voters. Most blacks in the country did.

The reporters were waiting outside the courthouse in clusters, and her supporters held a victory party at the home of an influential black businessman, but she extricated herself as quickly as possible and headed back to her family, gathered at Pie's. They all sat up until the wee hours, glorying in the victory, wondering at the implications of the coup, and guessing at what Mama and Papa would have had to say about it all. Jane was confident Papa would have been ecstatic, but Mama's reaction was not so clear to her. She only hoped she could "make them proud," as Mama was wont to say.

Chapter XII

Congratulations arrived in every form. Letters, telegrams, phone calls poured in from all corners of the globe. Her opponent never added his to the burgeoning list, however; she and he never spoke again. He served his term out without fanfare and practically no action. He had his chief deputy clean out the office before her swearing in, and he and his wife moved to their condominium on the beach in Destin, Florida. With the rampant corruption she had observed in his administration, Jane was confident they could afford the easy life.

The threats to her and her circle trickled down to nothing. There was a new look of respect on the faces of friend and foe alike when she moved about now. She worked to convince herself that all the enmity was behind her and all the county's citizens were her constituents, but she sometimes caught herself wondering if a suddenly friendly being had been "fer" or "agin" during the hotly contested race.

She and Donny spent a great deal of time planning for her tenure and deciding on a competent, impartial staff who could best serve all the citizens. She depended a great deal on Donny's knowledge of the people and the problems he knew to be unique to the area. Again, she was so thankful for him — how many times had that been the case in her life?

Before taking office there was one mission she had to complete. So, three days after the election, she flew to New York, unannounced, with a list of reasons Bill's parents should allow her to move Bill's body and that of their baby to her homeland. She was prepared for a fight and had all her arguments rehearsed. This unfinished business was the only thing which had disturbed her sleep since her victory, and now she was determined to have it resolved. She shouldn't have been concerned, however. Her in-laws readily agreed and wished her Godspeed. She honestly felt they were relieved to be free of the burden of caring for the graves.

She had optimistically made burial arrangements before booking the flight. So, two weeks before Jane Ellen Robbins Hammond became sheriff, Donny and Sadie, a small gathering of her family, and their minister gathered with her to welcome Bill and little Bill to their midst. With Bill's grave by Papa's, the two men she had loved most dearly lay eternally side by side, with the baby to the left of Bill and to the right of the spot already marked off for her.

The January morning of her swearing-in ceremony dawned cool and sunny. Not a single cloud was visible as she arose early, bathed, dressed, and drove to the cemetery to "visit" with her loved ones there. She told nobody where she would be. This was her time alone to tell them about what she was feeling and how she wished for their presence. She had a gut-wrenching cry as she stood in the rather expensive suit she had bought especially for the occasion and ended up wiping off most of the makeup she had so painstakingly applied earlier. She had wanted the entire "look" intact for them, even though she knew that was impossible. She desperately missed them today.

She drove back to the cottage to reapply her makeup and recheck herself in the mirror before driving to Parkesville. Just before heading back out the door, she felt it coming and rushed to the bathroom to throw up, as she had done all her life when she was this nervous.

On the podium, with her left hand on Papa's old Bible, still marked with the yellowed tissue paper, she raised her right hand and pledged to uphold the office to which she had been elected. The crowd was quite a bit larger than normal. This ceremony was usually an exercise in retaining the old guard or replacing it with more of the same. The significance of the change could be discerned by the difference in the composition of the gathering. For the first time ever, blacks outnumbered whites, and women also made up an impressively larger percentage of the group. Jane hoped and prayed all was for the betterment of this place she loved so. The next day she was at her office at 7:00 A. M. to make it begin to happen.

She only thought she had worked hard before! The office was in total disorder. Records were sketchy or missing entirely, funds were unaccounted for or misappropriated, equipment was outdated or nonexistent, and no job descriptions were evident anywhere. Deputies were accustomed to working autonomously, never accounting to anyone. Hence, bribery ran unchecked. After only a week, it became clear to the staff (that she had formed by retaining some and hiring some anew) that Sheriff Jane, as she preferred to be called, would not be doing things as they had been done before. The assistants could get with her program or get out. One young man jumped ship, but three other deputies, including Donny, elected to stay and try to make a difference.

All staff committed themselves to really long days at first, until things could be sorted out and straightened up. So it was only three weeks into her administration, after a twelve-hour day and with only three hours' sleep that Jane got the call that would reunite her with Lynn after twenty-eight years.

In a dazed state, she reached for the phone and noted the time on the digital clock. 3:27. Why didn't the dregs of society operate on a schedule akin of that of ordinary people?

Donny was at the other end of the line but was sketchy as to why she needed to come in immediately. That was normal.

Nobody gave out details on the phone. It was common knowledge that Mrs. DeMarkum listened in on cellular and cordless phone conversations. Rumors from unplanned pregnancies to alcoholic tirades traced their origins to that little electronic box on the table beside the old woman's recliner. For that reason, none of the locals dared say anything of importance over the wireless.

With a number of unanswered, unstated questions, Jane crawled from her warm bed and threw on a sweat suit. It was too late, too cold, and entirely unnecessary to worry about a uniform. That was for normal working hours. Besides, everyone recognized her without benefit of the badge. Recognized her, hell; she was the oddity of the century around here. Perhaps the oddity of all time.

Pulling on her coat over her pink sweats, she eyed her pistol in its holster draped over a chair and decided against taking it. Donny would have let her know if the situation were volatile. He hadn't. He had merely indicated that it was one that needed her immediate attention. That he asked her to meet him at her office rather than at the crime scene itself also implied no need of a weapon.

Abner eyed her as she left the room but never moved from his spot on the foot of her bed where she had thrown his afghan earlier in the evening.

As she started through the living room and kitchen to the garage, she hesitated as she felt a tingle run up her spine. Mama would have said, "A rabbit run over your grave," but she knew it was only the January draft from leaky old windows. Still there was more than a bit of apprehension as she left the warmth of her house, entered the cold garage, and put the key into the ignition.

The possibilities of what this case might be whirred through her mind as she drove. In an area where at least twenty-five percent were unemployed, fifty percent were functionally illiterate, and beer joints were ten times more prevalent than churches, fights, domestic disputes, public drunkenness, and theft were commonplace. Even during her short tenure, Jane had been roused from her bed three times before for professional reasons. It had been her experience, both here and in the North, however, that such occurrences were usually reserved for Friday, Saturday, and occasionally Sunday nights. That this was a Wednesday night, actually Thursday morning, didn't help her to zero in on the task that lay ahead.

Donny's car was the only one out front as she pulled into her parking slot. Must not be much need of backup. Her instincts, backed by more than twenty years' experience, told her that was a good sign. When she opened the door, she knew her assumption had been wrong.

Her chief deputy was alone in the office, and his pacing as well as the look on his face spoke volumes before he opened his mouth. She trusted his intuition; he had been a law officer as long as, actually longer than, she and was very good at his profession. That was one of the reasons he had earned the top spot. That he was her dear friend and one of the best men she had ever known was the other.

Before the door closed behind her, Donny was across the room, eyes wide. "Jane, it's Zell Green. He's dead. And it looks like Lynn did it. She finally had enough and shot him. I sent Simp on over there. I knew you didn't need to go alone. Hope you don't mind if I drive you."

She heard the words he uttered, but their meaning escaped her. It was impossible. Not sweet, gentle Lynn.

Donny climbed in under the steering wheel of her Blazer, and they began the six-mile trip out into the country to the house Zell and Lynn moved into after their marriage nearly thirty years earlier—the old home place of Miss Hattie's family. Jane recognized Zell's pickup truck, Lynn's older model Lincoln, and Miss Hattie's even older Cadillac when she and Donny pulled into the circular driveway. Seth's county car was on the north side of the house. The crowd hadn't started gathering yet, but they would. With or without Mrs. DeMarkum's detection device, there were those who always sensed where the stench lay.

Donny had apparently already called the coroner before she reached the office because his station wagon was turning off the gravel road and heading down the oak-lined drive just as Donny drove her up to the front steps.

Alighting from the vehicle, Jane realized this was her first trip to this house. She had never been, even as a girl, though it was only three or so miles from Mama and Papa's. She had ridden past it hundreds of times on her way to and from the little white clapboard AME church another two miles down the dirt road, but she had shunned even a furtive glance in its direction since that awful day shortly after her fourth birthday.

She did remember Mama's talking about what a shame that the once beautiful house had deteriorated. It had once been a showcase estate, boasting the hoof prints of General Sherman's horses that had run through its center dogtrot hall. But the headlights from her sports vehicle had given a preview of the desolation she now viewed up close. The large, spacious, one-story house with its wrap-around porch was in drastic need of repair.

The intricate gingerbread trim, once an absolute white, was now a faded gray indicating years of inattention. No paint had touched any of the building's exterior in quite some time.

Climbing the steps, with an anxious Donny at her side, Jane noted the loose board on the third level as well as the missing left corner of the top one. The front porch was in no better shape. A gaping hole at least a foot in diameter lay just to the right of the door.

The screen door squeaked as Donny pulled it open for her. It hung precariously on one hinge, the other only partially intact.

She wanted desperately to tuck tail and run as she entered what she had believed most of her life to be the abode of the Evil One incarnate. Jane had hated Mr. Till and Zell for almost as long as she could remember. Taking a deep breath, she resolutely walked into the front hallway where Seth met them and gave directions to the living room. There, just inside the door in a pool of his own blood, lay the late, great Zell Green. He had looked better. Half of his head was blown away, and what appeared to be the larger part of his brain was plastered on a dingy eggshell wall behind the body. A worn, yet otherwise impeccably clean Oriental rug also held its share of cranial contents.

Directly in front of Jane, Lynn was seated on a stiff, formal Victorian sofa. Nose bloody, lip split and swollen, a gash over her cheekbone, a look of total dejection in her eyes. The fact that the right side of her face was mangled and the left side unblemished gave her a surreal look. Something of a Salvador Dali effect.

In the room off to the right, Jane caught a glimpse of Miss Hattie as the older woman methodically filled the kitchen sink with water and gathered dirty dishes from a round oak table. She hummed some song whose tune Jane didn't recognize; seemingly oblivious to what was taking place in the adjoining room. The dim lighting afforded the sheriff little opportunity to observe the older lady's demeanor. The whole scene was straight out of a gothic novel.

Walking to the sofa, Jane sat and tentatively placed her arm around Lynn's shoulder. It had been a long time, and Jane didn't know what to expect or what to offer. The broken being that she hardly recognized embraced her and sobbed uncontrollably. Jane allowed Lynn the catharsis as the coroner, Doc Jones, and his assistant went about the work of examining the body.

Because she didn't want Lynn present for all the photos and probings that had to take place, and because she needed to so some probing of her own, Jane called to Miss Hattie, still in the kitchen, to ask for her help in getting Lynn to bed. Doc Jones would need to check her, too, before he left. Miss Hattie's eerie song never missed a beat, and the clinking of glasses in the sink never abated.

Easing her hands under Lynn's shoulders, Jane half led, half carried the limp form across the hall. Broken glass lined the floor, and Jane called to Donny to come and lift the barefoot Lynn. Having no idea of the layout of the house, Jane merely followed the path of destruction into the first door on the left.

Chaos was a mild term for the shambles! Covers were ripped from the four-poster bed and tossed all over the hardwood floor. A vase had smashed against the beveled mirror, the contents of the urn mixing with the shards of glass covering the antique dresser. A makeup case lay empty in a rocking chair, its holdings slung helter-skelter across the large room. And on the section of mirror left partially intact, fragments of lipstick-scrawled words spelled out "NIGGER LOVING BIT." Jane could feel the color rise in her cheeks as she mentally added the "ch" to the final word.

This room was no place for anyone to spend the night; particularly the obviously fragile Lynn.

Wending their way to the adjoining room whose lack of personal contents indicated a guest room, Donny and Jane got Lynn into bed. Going into what she had earlier noted to be a adjoining bathroom, Jane wet a cloth to wipe the woman's injuries and gasped at the image of herself in the mirror over the sink. The fear, pain, rage, and hatred she thought she had buried ages ago stared back at her. She splashed cold water on her face in a feeble attempt to wash away the expression before she reentered the room where her two dearest childhood friends awaited.

When she returned with the cloth, Lynn was already under the covers which Donny had obviously very efficiently arranged. A look of hurt in his eyes, he avoided hers. She knew he had read her thoughts as only loved ones can. Lynn's swelling had increased, and her nose was probably broken, but she managed to apologize in the midst of her suffering.

"Jane Ellen, I'm so sorry you had to see that. You know how Zell has always been. Filled with so much distrust and bitterness. Please accept my apologies on his behalf. This is my home, too, and I would do nothing to offend you or to make you feel unwelcome."

Jane made no comment as she hugged the small, frail shell of a woman who had once seemed so strong and confident. She wondered what Lynn's life could possibly have been like all those years. She also wondered at Lynn's references to Zell as if he were still alive. Apparently the reality of the night's events had not yet fully registered.

The obligatory questions could wait. Maybe with the help of Doc's injected sedative, Lynn could get some sleep, knowing she was now without further threat of physical harm.

Chapter XIII

After Lynn had been put to bed and left to Doc's expert care, Jane and Donny joined Seth in the living room to gather all the evidence they could. The investigation was really a matter of going through the motions.

Apparently, Zell had died at the hand of his wife, after a drunken tirade on his part. It must have been a doozy, given the condition of the bedroom and of Lynn's face. She had taken one beating too many at the hands of an abusive husband and had finally decided to do something in her own defense. From her years of professional observations of such relationships, Jane speculated that this was probably the first time Lynn had ever stood up to him in any way.

Seth showed her the apparent death weapon, a .38 caliber pistol. It was probably identical to a hundred others kept in bedside tables in as many households in this rural area. He placed the revolver and the three spent cartridges in a plastic zip-lock bag. The victim's body had been zipped into a much larger plastic bag earlier and was already on its way to the forensics lab. An autopsy was the law.

His camera had been packed up when the coroner's assistant granted Jane's request to allow her to take some shots of Lynn's injuries. Quietly entering the room, Jane did not fully rouse a sedated Lynn. She got four photos without Lynn's ever opening her eyes.

The sheriff also checked the instant prints of the body to make certain every angle was evident so there would be no questions when the grand jury met in about a month. Not that she thought there possibly would or could be. No jury in the county would ever believe that Jane committed, or was even capable of committing, murder. It would be a clear case of simple self-defense, and no charges would be brought. Even though Jane knew this, her extensive training and many years in police work would allow her to be nothing but thorough. Besides, there was the ever perfectionist Donny rechecking each detail.

It was 5:30 in the morning when they started to head back to the office, and Jane peeked in on Lynn one more time before leaving. Just to make sure the sedative was doing the trick. The thin, beaten woman, barely visible under the covers, was sleeping soundly. Except for the yet blond hair, there was not one bit of evidence of the lively girl the sheriff had loved so long ago.

When they arrived back at the office, Jane insisted that Donny go home for a while and get a little sleep, but he refused just as she refused at his insistence. The drive back to Parksrville had been virtually a silent one. Periodically they would utter monosyllabic utterances and then retreat back into their private reflections—both about the night's occurrences and those of their connected childhoods.

Even with all the work yet to be done to make her office honest again and with the endless reports that had to be completed after the shooting, Jane still found time to visit Lynn that afternoon. She hadn't called first. She didn't want the trip to appear a question-and-answer session. She was merely following up and making sure Lynn was as well as could be expected, and she hoped she could comfort her by explaining something of the law and what would probably follow, as far as the grand jury was concerned.

When she arrived at the Green house, the yard was full of cars, but Miss Hattie's was not among them. Apparently, the older mistress of the house was away. When Jane knocked on the kitchen door, she was met by one of the neighbors from up the road. This one was one of the newly migrated, not among the original settlers.

Jane entered the room in which Miss Hattie had held her strange vigil only a few hours earlier and found the oak table bending under the weight of home-cooked food and a gaggle of women come to do what Southern women were famous for doing, comforting with their culinary skills and their presence.

When Jane inquired about Lynn's whereabouts, she was told that the two Mrs. Greens were at the funeral home making arrangements for the burial two days later—as soon as the lab released the body. Jane had completely forgotten how quickly white folks buried their dead. Blacks took much longer and made something of a celebration of it, welcoming friends and family from far and near who often stayed for days before the actual services. Mama's internment had followed five days after her death. Mourners and those come to console had drifted in and out for all five of those days and a couple of days after the funeral.

Mama's two brothers had preceded their sister in death, but all of the nieces, nephews, and grand nieces and nephews arrived from five different states, and they all had a wonderful time catching up on their various lives. Jane remembered how tired she had been on the plane ride back to the city after the long week and a half at home. But she had also been so consoled by the large numbers of people who had loved Mama, too, and who had taken the time to tell her and the rest of the family.

Jane bade the ladies in the Green kitchen farewell and asked that they let Lynn know that she had been by and would call on her and Miss Hattie again after the funeral. Only after leaving the house, did she realize the women, not knowing hers and Lynn's background, had probably misinterpreted the sheriff's presence.

As a part of the job description, it was her responsibility to provide an escort for funeral processions. Usually that duty was assigned to a deputy, but this one Jane kept for herself, for a number of reasons. She wanted to be there for Lynn, and this was the only reasonable way she knew how. Also, when old Zell made his last ride down the highways of their county, she wanted his escort to be that same "nigger gal" he had terrorized years before. There was definitely some poetic justice there, she thought. So, in her dress uniform standing beside her official car as the short procession turned into the Baptist Church parking lot, she removed her hat and placed it over her heart, as was the custom here, and wondered what was going through the minds of the few who braved the cold rain to bury the bastard. Her presence had to be a bane to Zell's true friends, if there were any, and she prayed that the dearly departed was also aware of her. Then she agonized, if only momentarily, over her selfishness and shamelessness.

Donny had tried his best to talk her out of this detail, but she had made up her mind, and there was no changing it. There was not the level of satisfaction she had expected to experience, however. As a matter of fact, she was downright depressed by it. From her position in the back seat of the rental limousine, Lynn had looked so frail, withdrawn, and bruised. Also, there was poor Miss Hattie seated beside her who had not had very good luck with the men in her life either and who stared straight ahead with no sign of emotion whatsoever.

Chapter XIV

The notoriety of her election had waned somewhat as events across the country propelled other blacks to positions of prominence, and news services followed more alluring stories than hers. Because of that, the fact that the outside world got word of Zell's death was something of a surprise.

Normally, nothing to implicate one of their own ever made its way from the inner circles of the locals, They might malign each other, and often did, but would be damned if anyone else did! And they welcomed the media as they would a bed of rattlesnakes.

The local county newspaper printed Zell's obituary listing in its regular weekly edition the Wednesday following his death. A summary of the sheriff department's weekly activities also had an entry. That was it. Cause of death was not given, and no detailed report of the events was to be found between its paper's covers. Nobody expected there to be any other coverage. That was the way it was done. Neither Lynn nor Zell was to be denigrated.

So, when the first reporter from *Montgomery Advertiser* was waiting at her office after she returned from the funeral duties, Jane was not quite prepared. Although in retrospect, she realized she should have been. She refused an in-depth interview, but one of her, Tommy Ransom, supplied the media with a furtive conversation at a local café after office hours. She had considered relieving the young informant of his post right after she took office. He was not locally born and bred, but his family had been a part of the influx that moved in with the electrical systems factory He had stayed behind after the plant's closing to marry a local girl. He didn't always understand the unwritten code of the area, and Jane had been afraid that fact would come back to haunt them both. Now it had, and relieving him of his job at that point would be out of the question and of no use. She was left to deal with his opening of Pandora's box as best she could.

Sunday's paper ran colored pictures of a bruised Lynn and of the death scene itself, without benefit of the victim's mangled form, across the front page. Jane was livid. How the only photos in existence found their way from county possession to a newspaper spread was merely conjecture. When her staff saw the wrath with which she approached the discovery of the perpetrator, not one dared to offer any assistance. They were terrified of being labeled an accomplice.

Without explanation but with plenty of ideas as to the mole, Jane was forced to deal with the barrage of reporters. The phone and FAX lines stayed busy at all times, and answering machines at work and at home were full of messages each time she checked.

The wire services had picked up the story early on, and the same reporters who had followed her campaign were again pounding the pavement and hanging out at their earlier haunts. In most instances, they were nice enough and had actually received a better than lukewarm welcome on their previous quest. This time, however, their reception was not quite so hearty. They were asking questions that indicated guilt on the part of some of their own, and unpopular though Zell might have been, he was not be censured outside the locale. And the mere idea of speaking evil against Lynn could not be tolerated. Besides, there was Zell's poor old mother, Miss Hattie, to consider.

Accounts of Lynn's family background and their financial fall soon found their way into the stories which were the cover features in every weekly news publication, and Jane ached when Miss Pat's and Mr. George's good names were dragged through the mire alongside those of the Greens. Of course, the fact that Mr. Till had been responsible for Papa's death had been a leftover fact from the election newsgathering and made for interesting twists among the notable periodicals. Naturally, the tabloids had a field day with their convoluted interpretations.

The century-old courthouse stood in the center of the town square, which served as the gathering place for the press. Because the sheriff's office, a one-story modern metal building sporting a yellow brick facade, stood adjacent to the square, Jane could peer from her front window at the vultures awaiting any word coming from either the beautiful antebellum structure or its ugly antithetical, anachronistic afterthought.

Lynn had not been brought in on the night of the incident and would never be. And the grand jury met only twice a year; its next convening approximately five weeks away. So, nothing was happening of real interest now. What did they expect here? The reporters had gotten the background smut from Tommy and the bastard with the photos, whoever that was, but no one had offered any assistance after the sheriff's rage with the two rats became common knowledge.

Jane almost felt sorry for the young naive news gatherers who still wore their "Sunday best," as the locals would say, each day in vain hopes of even a fleeting moment in the TV camera's eye. The older, more jaded crew had begun to dress for comfort, but their designer-emblazoned clothing and expensive shoes made them easily discernible from the usual ingress and egress of the working class at public buildings.

The sheriff had noticed, with not the slightest trace of compassion, that soft drinks and nonperishables from one of the two general merchandise stores or the one gas station on the square was the fare. Nobody dared leave a spot long for fear that something about the case might be revealed in his or her absence.

Jane immensely enjoyed watching fastidiously manicured females and immaculately attired young males rip the easy-open tops off potted meat and Vienna sausage cans for a meal she had relished as a youngster but which must seem as foreign to them as Beluga caviar would be to most folks in these parts. She chuckled when she remembered overhearing the most fastidious of all the young women ask for Vienna sausage only to have the storekeeper roll his eyes at her pronunciation. These Yankees didn't know the "i" in "Vienna" was long and the following "e" long also.

Two weeks into their vigil, the modern-day carpetbaggers (Donny's term) with their carpet bags of attaches of leather and exotic skins, began systematically breaking camp and moving on to more fertile news fields with more sensational drama.

Jane noted the progression of the story in the newspapers from the front page of the first day to the bottom corner of the state news the last couple of days and knew it was becoming old goods, thankfully! She watched the final camera packed into its case and saw the most doggedly aggressive of the young reporters slip his pen into its legal pad holder and pull out for his California base.

A collective sigh of relief went through the sheriff's office as all looked forward to resuming business as usual. Tempers had been on edge all around the community as the populace felt on display at all times. Jane wondered what Lynn and Miss Hattie's life had become during this part of the ordeal. There had been no contact because Lynn's phone had been disconnected, and Jane feared the suspicion of impropriety if she were seen at the Green house. She would make a trip out there first thing tomorrow, she assured herself, to see how the ladies were doing.

That night she went home, bathed, and went to bed without even eating. She could never recall being so tired. The last two weeks had been the most physically and emotionally exhausting in a long time. She slept without so much as a recollected dream and awakened the next morning more refreshed than she had believed possible. As soon as she thought Donny might be up, she dialed his number. Sadie answered. The sound of her friend's voice was comforting.

"Sadie, hope I didn't get you up."

"Are you kidding!" Sadie assured her. "Since Donny turned fifty he's up before dawn every morning exercising away old age. He does look good, though, for an old man, don't you think?"

"Well, to be perfectly honest," Jane confessed, "for the last few weeks I haven't noticed much of anything. Praise God, maybe we're out of the limelight for a while now, though. If your youthful husband can tear himself away from his regimen, I'd like to speak to him, please."

"Sure, I'll get him," Sadie assured her. "Come by and see us, Jane. It's been too long. We've missed having you around since you got so busy with all this mess. Sara asked me the other day when you were coming back to see us. She left one of the baby's newest pictures for you."

Donny and Sadie's Sara was married to a young man Jane liked a lot, and they lived in Montgomery where they both taught elementary school. They were the parents of a three-month-old son, Jane's godson. She felt a pang of guilt at not being as active a member of their lives as she had intended. She would now, she silently promised herself.

The gut-wrenching pain she had felt after the loss of her only child had given way, over the years, to a dull ache that never quite left. She was so appreciative to Donny and his family for the opportunity to be an active part of the lives of their children and grandchildren. The honor of being named godparent to the first one born after her return was almost overwhelming. She had certainly done her share of spoiling him but realized that lately she had not been so generous with her time. She assured herself she would begin rectifying that omission immediately.

"You tell that lovely creature that I'll be by to see them sometime next week; I'll call first. I want to take her and little Donny shopping for his three-month birthday present. We've all got to get together soon and start planning a graduation party for the youthful Mr. Donny, Sr. Next time you talk to Brad, mention it to him and see when he can take off to get home."

Brad was Donny and Sadie's other child, a senior in undergraduate school at Emory. He had earned an academic scholarship following high school and, based on his grades while in college, had retained it all four years. Come fall, he was entering medical school at the University of South Alabama in Mobile and was a fine young man.

"I'll do it, Jane. I talked to him last night. He's studying really hard this semester, but he's had time to be concerned about you and his daddy the last several weeks. He's read all the newspaper stories. Said it made him something of a celebrity, though. He thought it might be a real girl magnet. Still looking for Miss Right, you know." Sadie teased.

"She'll find him. Anybody as sweet, as smart, and as good looking as he is won't have a problem. His only dilemma will be sortin' 'em all out," Jane joked.

"Thank you, Jane. We're extremely proud of both our children, but it's always nice to have someone else recognize how wonderful they are, even if that someone isn't exactly unbiased either. I'll get started on the planning stages of the graduation bash. Only six more weeks before the law degree, but Donny won't discuss it for fear of jinxing it. He is obsessed with the bar exam. You know he can't accept anything less than perfection in himself. I can't imagine him failing after the way he's attacked school and with the grades he's earned, but he'll worry himself to death until he knows for sure. You know how he is. And I think he still finds it hard to believe a poor kind from the Bottom actually made it, "a proud Sadie mused.

Donny, always the driven one, had been going to school all his life, he said. He had gotten his undergraduate degree in criminal justice at night, sometimes while working two jobs. With his diploma came an increase in salary, negating the need for multiple employment. Two years later he had returned to night school, and two years after that had a master's degree. Three years ago, he had decided to pursue a law degree, and with near perfect grades was about to accomplish his latest goal for himself. It had been far from easy. With a demanding job, a family he adored, and difficult law courses, he had become an expert at juggling his time and surviving on little sleep. Jane had never heard him complain, though, and had little patience for those who bellyached constantly.

Jane and Sadie had been talking about a party in honor of this, hopefully last, graduation, for some time, but Donny was opposed, or so he pretended. Said he didn't need any accolades nor trumpet fanfare.

"He's going to bear with us," Jane told Sadie. A graduation party it is. We'll have another one when he passes the bar. Mr. Serious will just have to relax a little bit and enjoy this milestone. It deserves recognition."

"Agreed, Jane. Just a minute. I'll get Donny." Sadie pretended to move the phone as she offered for Jane's hearing, "Donny, it's that old battle ax boss you gripe about all the time. Oops, Sheriff, forgot you could hear me. That wasn't meant for your ear."

"Yeah, right," Jane returned the banter. "You'll get yours! Just wait till this old battle-ax gets down with the next duty roster. Mr. Tight Buns is gonna be on third shift every night he isn't in school!"

"Hey, boss," a rather chipper sounding Donny offered. "Lord, it's so good to hear somebody actually kidding a little bit. Everybody has been so tense for so long around here. I was beginning to think I'd never hear light conversation again."

Jane had thought the same thing while talking to Sadie. She learned to appreciate Donny's choice in women more and more with each passing day.

"What's got you up so early this morning?" Donny continued.

"Got a favor to ask you."

"Sure. Shoot."

"Hang out at the office and handle my duties till I get there. I think all the carpet baggers are gone, but watch for any stragglers snooping around, disguised as humans, and for Christ's sake, don't let any of the deputies say a word to anybody about anything, excluding, perhaps, the weather.

"I want to go see Lynn as soon as I think she might be up. I've waited as long as I can. I don't want anyone but you knowing where I am. Evade the question; lie if you have to, but don't tell a soul.

"If you need me, send somebody to get me, but in the meantime you're in charge. I trust any decision you might need to make."

"Great!" Donny quipped. "I just decided I need a week off with pay."

"Forget that, Pal. I need you and your legal mind. When all this is over, and the grand jury has rendered a decision, then we'll all take some time off, but forget a week; we'll be lucky to get a day each," Jane warned.

"You are a battle ax!" I can't believe I signed on for this," Donny pouted.

"Oh, you love it, and you know it. Thanks, though, Donny. It's good to know I can always depend on you," a grateful Jane said.

"Always glad to help a friend. But are you sure you can do this yourself? You know I'll go with you," Donny offered.

"I know that and appreciate the offer, but maybe next trip. After all the years of estrangement, I think this visit needs to be mine alone. I shouldn't be long. See you when I get back to the office."

"Take your time. It'll give me a chance to feel bossy and important like you women are always doing, for a change. But be careful. Don't bite off more than you can chew - emotionally, I mean. You don't have to make up for all the years of bad blood all at once. You two have the rest of your lives to work out your relationship. And if I know either of you like I think I do, you'll get it done," a wise Donny contributed.

"Yea, I know, but I've got to see about Lynn, Donny. I've felt guilty most of my adult life about her, and now she must think I've abandoned her again. Got to start trying to rectify all that."

"Okay, do it your way, Donny conceded, "but you know we love you. Just be careful."

"Thanks. I needed that affirmation. I know y'all do, and I love y'all, too. I'll check my emotions at the door and just be professional," Jane promised.

"Now that's the biggest joke or lie you've told since I've known you. See you in a little while, Boss."

Jane drove back home, took a quick shower, and drank two cups of strong coffee as she read the morning paper, which blessedly contained no mention of Landes County or its residents. She couldn't remember when she had felt so contented. She was a bit nervous about facing Lynn again, but she also found herself excited about the possibility of renewing their friendship. Nothing would please her more, but she realized there were variables over which she again had no control. Nevertheless, she would certainly do what she could.

Chapter XV

Lynn was in a pink velour robe and pink terry cloth scuffs when she let the sheriff in the back door. There was a bit of deja vu as Jane's mind rushed back to their first meeting in another kitchen when the little hostess wore pink then, too. That's where the similarities of the two times ended.

While her facial injuries were obviously healed after so long a time, there was a fresh scar over her right eye and an old one on her neck that looked as if it might have been caused by a burn. Lynn's robe was faded and threadbare, and her right shoe was separating at the sole seam right at her big toe. The room was cold, and Jane wondered if the ladies could afford sufficient heat. She remembered the phone's disconnection and thought perhaps it was for nonpayment rather than a protection of privacy, as she had earlier supposed it to be.

Lynn's facial expression as she answered the door revealed nothing of her feelings, and Jane was hesitant to reveal any emotion, either. Maybe she really had deferred her feelings, as she had promised Donny she would. However, the pause, seeming immense, was actually only a miniscule one before Lynn reached for Jane and gave her a heartfelt hug. With utter relief and abandonment, Jane returned the embrace, and both women released a floodgate of pent-up baggage in a barrage of tears. When they finally withdrew from the embrace and each surveyed the other, Jane was not pleased with what she saw but tried not to let her face disclose that. It was Lynn who broke the silence.

"Jane Ellen, you can't know how happy I am that you are finally here. I have waited so long to see you and to talk to you."

"I know how much I've missed you," a tearful Jane admitted. "I'm so sorry I haven't been back the last two weeks, but I didn't want a bunch of outsiders who don't understand the situation trying to make something out of my being here. I felt like I had to wait until I didn't need to sneak around."

"Well, of course you did," an understanding Lynn offered. "We've had enough to deal with from the reporters since that awful night. There was one young man waiting here at the house when Miss Hattie and I got back from the funeral. He pretended he was a relative from out of town. The young girl who had stayed here, Betty, is new to the area and didn't know he was lying. He jumped on us the minute we walked through the door until some of the neighbors politely asked him to leave and then got downright insistent on it after he initially refused. He left in a huff, and that first bit of garage hit the front page of the paper the next day. I read that article but haven't picked up a newspaper or a magazine since.

"I tried to keep Miss Hattie from knowing anything about the press coverage, but I completely forgot about the T.V. news and came into the room two days after the funeral to find her bawling while a shot of her son's body flashed across the screen. She has been practically bedridden ever since. It is so unfair to her. She understood how he was, but she was his mother, and he was her only child. I just wish I could protect her from all this. She says she'll never be able to leave the house again, and she enjoyed her church activities and her bridge club so much.

"Jane Ellen, I've completely forgotten my manners," Lynn continued. "Please sit down and talk to me while I fix us some breakfast. You will eat with me, won't you?"

"I've already had coffee this morning, but that would be nice."

"What will my future be? Will I have to go to jail?" an obviously worried Lynn inquired as soon as Jane was seated.

"I wouldn't think so," Jane assured her. "From what I've seen and heard since Zell's death, and really ever since I moved back, I'd think most folks know what your life has been like, and the grand jury, made up of those same folks, won't bring charges. Of course, that is purely speculation, but I still believe I know the people around here well enough to predict how they'll respond. The pictures Seth took of you after the beating you obviously took that night should convince anyone."

"Oh, Lord," Lynn bemoaned. "How embarrassing to have our dirty laundry aired so graphically. Will it be necessary to show the pictures, do you think?"

"Lynn, whether we show the pictures or not, what happened that night will have to come out. What he did to you then and all the times before that night is your defense. Besides, Honey, I don't suspect there is a person in this county who will see a single snapshot in court that he or she hasn't pored over at length in his own home from the pages of some publication. Your dirty laundry has already been aired before the whole world by the media. For that I owe you another apology. The pictures leaked out sometime early on by God knows who. I've tried to find out, but nobody has come forward with even a clue after my staff learned how out of control I was about the whole thing.

"I have a feeling it was that snotty-nosed Ramsey boy. I kept him on as a deputy, against my better judgment. You know the one. He married the Smith girl from the Bottom."

When Lynn looked quizzical, Jane continued." The Smith girl who had the twin brother who drowned in the rock pond last Fourth of July. I know Ramsey's the one who talked to the first reporters, and I have a gut feeling he got his hands on the evidence negatives and sold them. If I can prove it, he's history. I've been needing an excuse to fire him, anyway!" an angry Jane stated firmly.

"First of all, you don't owe me an apology," Lynn assured her. "Of course you didn't mean for any of this to happen, but it would have been made public sooner or later. Most people love following this sort of thing. And as for that poor Ramsey boy, go easy on him. He's had a rough time of it. His mother was sick with cancer when they left here after the plant closed. She died a short time afterward. His daddy started drinking heavily after losing the plant job, and Tommy became responsible for the family. He has a younger brother and sister he supported for years until they were old enough to make a living for themselves. He probably still helps with his daddy's upkeep. I'm sure he did this without malice. He just needed the money, I would imagine. Probably didn't even think it could cause anybody pain."

Jane was ashamed of her bitterness toward Tommy when she heard nothing but compassion for him and his plight from the one person whose life he had so adversely affected. So like Lynn to look past her own troubles to those of others, just as Miss Pat always did. Nevertheless, Jane knew she herself was not nearly so generous and knew that from this day forward, Tommy either toed the mark or looked for another job.

At that moment there was a knock on the door, and Lynn lowered the flame on the stove while she answered it. She greeted the visitor with warmth, and both he and Jane were shocked when Pie strode into the room and they spotted each other.

"Good morning, Jane," her cousin stumbled to say. "What are you doing here so early, and where is your car?"

"Hello, Pie," answered an equally stumbling Jane. "The car is out back behind the fence in case any of the news mongers are still around. What are you doing here?" Before the last words had escaped her lips, Jane realized that was not a question she really had any right in asking and deeply regretted voicing it.

Pie did not seem offended, however. "I just came by to see what Miss Hattie and Lynn might need today." Turning to his hostess, "How about it, Lynn"

"Thank you so much, Pie, but we're okay for now, I think."

Jane got the distinct impression that this was not the first time Pie had offered his services when Lynn continued. "The groceries you brought yesterday will hold us for a while. Won't you stay and have a cup of coffee with us, though?"

"No thanks, Lynn. I've got to get on to work. I'll check on y'all tomorrow. Oh, almost forgot. You and Miss Hattie didn't have any mail. Bye, Jane, I hope we'll be seeing you for dinner soon." And with that, Pie was gone, leaving Jane more than a little confused.

Lynn turned the flame back up on the stove and resumed her cooking with no indication that the man's appearance was the least bit unusual. It was a moment before she broke the silence. "For Miss Hattie's sake, I absolutely detest all this public attention. I never loved Zell; so his memory is not an issue with me, and I think I quit feeling for myself after both my parents had died. I hate their good names have been dragged around for ridicule by people who didn't know what fine people they were. But I knew what they were like, and everybody who really matters to me does, too. But poor Miss Hattie! She has been so good to me. I couldn't have made it all these years without her. But even though she knew his faults, Zell was her son, and she couldn't do one thing to stop his evil bent. She tried."

Finally Jane found an opening to satisfy her curiosity concerning her cousin's presence. "Does Miss Hattie know that Pie is coming around here? Surely with what's happened between our two families, she wouldn't approve of his being on the place. I even worried about what she would think when she found out I had come by. I don't mean to sound crass, but I'm really surprised that Pie chooses to help y'all, too."

"Jane Ellen, Miss Hattie has a great deal of respect for you and for the rest of your family. She was so excited when you were elected sheriff. Of course I was the only one she confided that to, but she thought it was amusing that Zell carried her to the polls where she pulled the lever for you. Bless her heart, not much in her life has been cause for laughter, either."

Turning from the stove to face Jane, Lynn continued. "As far as Pie is concerned, he has been seeing about the two of us for years. There is no room in that big heart of his for any ill will toward anyone. Oh, he wasn't exactly fond of Zell, but that was a sentiment he shared with a rather large segment of the population."

After all the bad blood, literally and figuratively, Jane had never dreamed that there was now, or had been, any contact between her family and the Greens. And that anybody in this household had actually voted for her was actually beyond her comprehension. She wondered if Lynn had voted at all, but she could never broach that subject. "That thrills me more than you could ever know, Lynn. I always thought Miss Hattie was nice, and Mama thought a lot of her, even after Papa's death. I couldn't understand that then, but maybe I was too young."

"Yeah, you were. There were a lot of things neither one of understood. We did understand that we were best friends, though, didn't we? We just didn't know how good those early times together were."

"I probably knew more than you. I thought I had died and gone to heaven when you welcomed me into your home and into your family immediately on that first day Mama and I walked up the hill," Jane reminisced.

At that point, Lynn set the table for two and placed a plate of biscuits and a bowl of "pap" gravy out. Growing up, Jane's family had eaten the meatless concoction, also known by locals as "zuzu," or "sawmill," gravy when the money had run out, and the pork from hog killing was gone or extremely low. Prepared with flour browned in grease and thinned with water, it was often a staple of the truly destitute. Sometimes in New York, she had cooked it as comfort food when she longed for home. But she knew a guest in the home would have warranted Lynn to cook something more substantial if she had had it. They weren't merely poor; Miss Hattie and Lynn obviously had nothing.

"Isn't Miss Hattie joining us?" Jane managed to ask.

"No, she'll be in bed until much later. I'll take her something after a while—when she wakes up. It's just the two of us for breakfast, Jane Ellen, just like it used to be. How many meals do you suppose we've shared?" inquired Lynn as she sat facing her friend.

"Not enough!" Jane quickly retorted.

"Agreed, Jane Ellen."

While they ate and drank hot, but weak, coffee, the two moved to much less serious topics and actually shared a laugh or two before Jane looked at her watch and realized it was already nearly ten. She had not intended to stay this long. She hoped and prayed everything was all right at the office. She knew she could trust Donny, but she didn't want to put undue pressure on him. He was really worried about finishing law school and passing the bar exam, even with his exemplary grades and excellent study skills. Besides, there might be some hotshot reporter slipping back in for any snippet of information; so she ended the pleasant meeting.

"Lynn, I have to go, but I'll be back," Jane promised. "Whatever we have to do, we can not lose each other again. Will you let me cook supper for you sometime?"

"I'd love that, Jane Ellen, but I'll have to make arrangements. I can't just leave Miss Hattie alone. She depends on me totally," Lynn said.

"Are you sure that's it, Lynn, and not what the community will think if you visit in my home?" a still suspicious Jane queried.

"Jane Ellen, I've spent most of my life complying with and following the rules that this area established, and look where that got me," Lynn affirmed. "If I can get Miss Hattie settled in so that I feel she is safe and secure, I'll be there whenever you invite me, with bells on!"

"Friday night at seven o'clock. I'll run by after work to make sure you can make it," Jane arranged.

Jane left the run-down house and its cold kitchen with a greater warmth and a lighter step than she had possessed in years.

The following Friday night, the two of them again sat around a table sharing a meal—this time in Jane's cozy cottage with Abner a third presence. He and Lynn hit it off immediately, and he didn't venture far from her feet the entire evening.

Jane had spent hours planning and preparing the food. She had made lists, revised them, thrown them out entirely, and started anew a number of times in an effort to prepare the sorts of things they had shared as young girls. She also tried, as best she could, to duplicate Mama's techniques. While she was certain that was impossible, since Mama never followed a recipe in her life—partly because of her illiteracy and partly because that's how she had learned from her mother—the result was worth the work Jane had expended. The fried pork chops, buttermilk biscuits, collard greens, candied sweet potatoes, cracklin' bread, potato salad, and bread pudding were delicious, if she said so herself.

Lynn raved on and on about how good it all was, and she certainly ate her share. Jane was not sure she had ever seen such a small woman eat so much. Of course, that only served to increase Jane's concern about the finances and welfare of her friend, but the time still wasn't right to mention it. Instead, they talked, primarily, about old times and their fun days together.

"Remember, Jane, Ellen," Lynn mused and quickly apologized, "I know it's 'Jane' now to most people, but I'm having a hard time remembering that; give me time, but do you recall how we used to sneak away from Mother and your grandmother and go to the old clay pit where we molded the dirt into cones on the end of sticks? Then we'd lick it off like ice cream cones? Pie taught us how."

"I reckon I do!" Jane exclaimed. "I think I've still got the marks on my legs from the switching I got the day you didn't wipe quite all of it off your mouth before going home. Mama had a fit when she saw it. Said eating clay was all right for us, but white younguns weren't supposed to be doing such. Said most whites didn't believe it was clean. I think she was afraid you would get into trouble with your folks because of Pie and me. She cleaned you up completely before your parents saw you. That was another of those times when I didn't understand the unwritten rules. Mama didn't take time to explain before she tore me up, either! She believed in the power of that dirt, though. You know she had Pie and me get her some to eat the day before she died."

"Oh, I felt so guilty when you got that whipping because of me, and so guilty not doing anything when Macy died," Lynn confessed. "I didn't even get in touch with any of y'all. You know she was like a grandmother to me, too, when we were growing up, and my parents loved her so."

"Nobody expected you to do anything, Lynn. We all understood what your life had become. Everybody knew Zell and his bigotry. To be honest, I was surprised to get your card when Bill died. I appreciated it so much."

"Yet another time when I felt so guilty, Jane Ellen, and wanted to call and talk to you, but Zell paid all the bills, and he checked the phone bills especially carefully. Toward the end of their lives, I was not even allowed to call my parents. He said it was because it was long distance and a waste of money since they visited me once a week, but I think it was just another way he could control me."

"I was surprised that you knew about Bill at all," Jane stated, "and certainly about his death."

"Miss Hattie kept up with you almost on a daily basis after your folks got the phone. She and Macy were a great deal of comfort to each other, especially after Macy got so sick and was bedridden," Lynn explained.

"I had no idea that Mama and Miss Hattie kept in touch, and certainly not so closely," a shocked Jane uttered. "Why didn't anybody tell me?"

"Your Mama and Miss Hattie both knew the score around here. A white woman and a black woman were not supposed to be close except as employer/employee. Pie, Dot, your Uncle Jack and Aunt Laura Mae, and I knew, and we all also knew to keep our mouths shut. We agreed it was for your own good not to involve you. You were a long way from home at the time and would have worried.

"One time Zell came home from the store earlier than usual to get a bottle of whiskey he had hidden the night before and caught his mother on the phone with Macy. He went absolutely berserk when he figured out who was on the other end of the line. He ripped the phone out of the wall while they were still talking. It was two weeks before we had service again because Miss Hattie was embarrassed to contact the phone company. Your folks sneaked around and checked on us daily to make sure we were safe, and finally Pie slipped in and repaired the line when he knew Zell was gone to Montgomery for the day.

"Zell never asked how it got fixed, and neither of us ever said anything about it again. The calls between the two women resumed immediately, though, and continued until you got home just before Macy's death.

"We kept up with practically everything you did after you moved away. Miss Hattie and I spent many long days together, virtual prisoners in our house, and you were often the main topic of conversation. We were so proud of your accomplishments at work and thrilled when we learned you were marrying somebody your family thought so highly of. We even saw pictures taken the Christmas before the wedding when you brought him home."

This was more than Jane could assimilate. "Lynn, how in the world could you have see pictures and have followed my life even before my folks had a phone without Zell's knowing about it?"

"We were dealing with two pretty crafty and determined women," Lynn reminded her. "They had worked out a system years earlier, during Mr. Till's lifetime, whereby Miss Hattie mailed letters and packages to your family every Friday when she went into Montgomery to buy the groceries for the week. She had a post office box in a fictitious name there where she also got correspondence from them. Mr. Till was always at the store working when she took her weekly trips to town and never suspected a thing. Oh, he watched her closely at home, but he underestimated her. He would never have believed she could defy him so."

"But Mama couldn't read and write," a yet confused Jane declared.

"Stump read all the correspondence until his death," Lynn attempted to clarify. "After Mr. Till killed him, first Jack, then Pie, accepted that responsibility. I didn't know anything about all that until Miss Hattie started depending on me more and more to see about her affairs as she got older and as Zell got more out of hand. It was gut-wrenching for her to tell me because she worried so about what Zell would do if he ever found out, but she knew how much I loved you and your family, and she needed to keep in touch with them. She had to trust me to keep her secret. And I never betrayed that trust."

"All this is mind boggling," Jane sighed. "Hers and Mama's relationship is more than I can grasp. That my surviving family knew about it and didn't let on to me is unforgivable! Did no one think I was capable of dealing with the situation?"

"Oh, heavens, no! You must never blame them or be angry with any of them!" Lynn beseeched. "Miss Hattie made each of them promise never to tell you because she knew your concern for me would prompt you to intercede and try to make contact. That could have meant Miss Hattie's death or mine. Zell would have killed one or both of us, I'm sure. All the secrecy was to protect us; blame me if think you've got to blame somebody."

"I refuse to waste any more time with any kind of negative feelings between you and me. It's just all so confusing and surprising. What is actually wrong with Miss Hattie now?" Jane wondered aloud.

"Nothing specific physically, although she is getting old. She has been in a terrible emotional state. Zell, bad as he was, was all the real family she had, and now he's gone. That's why she needs me so badly," Lynn offered.

"I'm sorry, Lynn. I hope because of loyalty to her, you don't feel guilty about his death. For all practical purposes, Zell destroyed himself. It wasn't your fault."

"Believe it or not, "Lynn confessed, "I don't feel anything concerning his death except relief that he's gone and concern for her. I'm so thankful I can take care of her. I'm all she has left, and I'm just an in-law."

"I'd say 'just an in-law' is an understatement. She is so fortunate that the one thing that Zell ever got right was you," Jane assured her.

"Thank you, Jane Ellen, but I'm lucky to have her, too. I don't have much left either, you know."

"I know. It broke my heart when Miss Pat and Mr. George died. And the fact that you had no children—was that planning on your part?" Jane quizzed. "You would have made such a good mother, and children could have been a great comfort."

"I never used any form of birth control," Lynn began. "Zell wanted desperately to have a son to carry on the wonderful tradition of males in his illustrious family. His father was insistent on it, too. He used to make snide, off-color remarks all the time, embarrassing me to tears. I got pregnant the second year we were married, and Zell and his daddy pitched some kind of drunk when I got home from the doctor with the news.

"About four months later, I miscarried after flying head over heels down the back door steps. Of course the 'accident' was no accident. He was mad because I didn't have his supper ready when he got home from the store. Miss Hattie usually caught the flack for the food not being right, but she was out of the house; so I was the lucky one that day.

"He really did a number on me at the bottom of the stairs, too. I never got pregnant again, thank God! I had to have a hysterectomy the next year, partially the result of that incident. I was so relieved. I couldn't bear the thought of exposing an innocent child to that life or of reproducing anything in that family.

I knew when you got pregnant, and we, Miss Hattie and I, followed your progress with such joy. We would finally have a baby we could safely love, if from a distance. I was devastated when I learned you had miscarried, too. So much pain for you to have to endure in such a short time. I knew

Sadie and Donny were going to you, and I wanted to contact them before they left—send my regards, but Miss Hattie wisely persuaded me not to. She didn't want to bring them into our entanglement for their protection and for fear any additional confidants could jeopardize everybody's safety."

"My God, Lynn, is there nothing you haven't endured?" Jane cried. "Why did your parents insist you marry that sorry bastard, anyway? Sorry, but I know how much they loved you and wanted only the best for you."

"No child could have ever been adored more than I was by my parents, but they believed that I had to have material things since they had provided so lavishly for me up to the time Daddy gave it up and admitted he couldn't pull himself out of the financial fiasco he ultimately found himself in.

"You believed you had no control over your life when you were growing up because of the color of your skin, but you really had as much as or more than I ever did. White Southern women of my social class were expected to marry Southern men of wealth, heritage, and position in the community and rear similar Southern men and women.

"We were to get a liberal arts education, know which fork and which glass to use, where to place the napkin during and after the meal, how to smile demurely and say nothing of importance about any subject, keep up appearances, and take excellent care of the house and the man of the house. When decent men of wealth and position ran out or time didn't permit a period of looking, the women were forced to settle for the nearest thing. Zell appeared to be that nearest thing for me when time was running out.

"Miss Hattie had been a friend of my family for years, and though I didn't know him well, I thought surely Zell could not be so bad with such a lovely mother. I knew he was a bigot, but a lot of people were then. I believed I could help him overcome that fault with what was considered rather liberal thinking on my part. I was dead wrong, but by the time I discovered that fact, we were already married. And the absolute worst thing a true Southern woman could do was divorce the lord of the manor, no matter how awful he might be.

"That's it in a nutshell. My parents were devastated when they saw what my life had become. My situation hastened their deaths, I'm sure. You know the really sad part? Long before that nice boy in college I wrote you about, I was in love with Donny," Lynn admitted.

"I never knew that, Lynn," a surprised Jane admitted, not even back then. I thought I knew your every thought."

"Of course I could never admit it, even to you. I hope Donny didn't know either. But as smart as he always was, he probably knew. I never said anything and tried to convince myself I didn't have feelings for him. He and his family were from the Bottom, and the only worse thing a girl in my position could have done would be admitting to caring for a black. Understand why I don't worry any more about the mores of this antiquated society?" Lynn explained.

"Have you and Donny remained friends?" Jane inquired. "He's never mentioned any sort of current relationship."

"Oh, no. I never corresponded after he left for Montgomery. Although I know you and he did, and I wished so much to be a part of the threesome again. Even after I got over loving him, I longed for the friendship. I understand his wife is really nice, and his children have done well. I'm so glad. Nobody ever deserved it more. And he's in law school, I heard."

"Sadie is wonderful and would love to get to know you. She is secure in their relationship and would welcome you into their family, as she has me. We'll all have to get together later, okay?" Jane asked.

"That would be fabulous, if you're sure. I've had no friends outside my household for what seems a lifetime," Lynn admitted. "I can't even imagine what it would be like for you, Donny, me to get together again."

"Then consider it done, Lynn," Jane assured her. "I'm sure Sadie would enjoy that, and Donny would be elated. He's been worried about you, too. We've discussed you and your circumstances several times."

"That's embarrassing," Lynn sighed. "Apparently everybody knew what my life was like, and we tried to hide it. Never air the dirty linen, you know."

"Let that be the least of your worries, Lynn. All that is behind you now. Something I still don't understand is Miss Hattie's attitude. If she is so good, and I believe she is, why did she ever marry Mr. Till? He was a bastard, too. Surely she couldn't have loved him."

"Same reason I married Zell. She was a Southern woman of wealth and position who was to marry a Southern man of wealth and position. The pickings were slim for her, too. The beat goes on around here."

"But why were she and Mama so close? Surely there were white women of her social strata she could have socialized with?" mused Jane.

"Of course there were, and she did, particularly at church, but hers and Macy's relationship went back a long way. It had undergone some real trials," Lynn tried to explain.

"Like Papa's death, for instance? How did their friendship possibly survive that?" Jane asked.

"That's something only Miss Hattie can explain."

"Do you think she would see me? I would like to apologize to her for my faulty reasoning toward her all those years and to talk to her about Mama and Papa. You know I don't even know what it was Papa was supposed to have done that would give Mr. Till cause to kill him," Jane wondered aloud.

"She would see you, I'm sure, but I'm not so sure that's such a good idea, Jane.(I got the name right!) You wouldn't correct your past with her by making life worse for her now," Lynn reasoned.

"Of course, you're right," Jane agreed. "I would just be sacrificing her in order to salve my conscience. Would you do me a favor, and tell her I asked about her? Also let her know I truly appreciate her concern for me and for my family all these years. I resented her kindness and generosity following Papa's death, and I know now that was wrong. Would you let her know all that for me?"

"I will, and I'm sure she'll be thrilled. She worried for so long that you didn't understand her part in the whole of things. She feared you grouped her in with the men in this family, and I can assure you nothing could be farther from the truth."

"I suppose for a while I did," Jane mused, "but I never hated her like I hated Mr. Till and Zell. My feeling for them was strong emotion born of repeated injustices at their hands. I hope now that both of them are dead, I can finally bury all that, too. I'm worn out from hauling it around."

"Another thing I've been having trouble mentioning—it doesn't take a genius to realize that y'all are having a hard time making it financially. We need some help with the bookkeeping at the office. If I can get it approved by the county commissioners, would you be interested in the job? You could do it. It's not technical. I remember how smart you are. Taught me to read. The pay wouldn't be great, but it would beat nothing."

"Nothing is pretty much what we have now. I would love to try it," Lynn said, "but again there is the matter of taking care of Miss Hattie."

"What if I brought the work to you on Friday afternoons and picked up the previous week's at the same time?" Jane offered. "You could work at your own pace and still be able to see about Miss Hattie."

"Jane, you are too kind," Lynn gushed. "That sounds perfect!"

"I can't promise anything for certain yet," Jane crawfished. "Give me time to present the idea. The commissioners meet next Tuesday night. It's a bunch of men, though, you know. Never know what they'll do."

"Still having trouble with the gender thing," Lynn chuckled.

"Years of training, I guess," Jane admitted. I've worked so hard to overcome the gender and the race issues. I just can't seem to turn them loose."

"You've overcome every obstacle you've ever faced. I'm so envious of you and what you've accomplished," Lynn confessed. "There's nothing you haven't achieved when you've set your mind to it. Your strength has been my salvation. When I felt that I had held on as long as I could and was ready to give up, I would think of you and all your feats and imagine I was with you, enjoying all your freedom and opportunities. Macy always let us know when you got a promotion, bought the house, changed jobs, everything. We were so eager to hear from you. We even knew each time you got a dog and what its name was. I knew old Abner here before I ever saw him."

"I can't quite grasp this, Lynn. I've believed for years that our lives were totally disconnected while mine was open to you all the time. I feel cheated that I didn't know what was going on with you. I still don't understand why the messengers couldn't carry the news both ways. We could have rekindled our friendship as soon as I got home," Jane lamented.

"No, we couldn't have!" Lynn was quick to affirm. "Zell would have killed you, Miss Hattie, and me. And you didn't need to know about my life anyway. It wasn't a pretty sight. No, you couldn't know. It wasn't safe. We've got the present, and I'm so thankful for that, but it couldn't have happened sooner.

"Oh, me, look at the time! I've got to get home and check on Miss Hattie. Thank you so much for the food and the conversation. This has been the nicest evening I've spent since my marriage. The meal was almost as good as Macy's, and you and I both know that's the supreme compliment for anybody's cooking,"

"Thank you, Lynn. I've wrapped up the leftovers for you and Miss Hattie to have tomorrow."

"She'll love that, and so will I. Thanks again, Jane," Lynn spoke as she reached for an embrace of her friend.

After Lynn's departure, Jane cleaned the kitchen and went to bed, but not to sleep. There were too many unanswered questions and questions that wouldn't quite form. She would go see Pie and Uncle Jack in the morning, but first she was going to see Mama and Papa again. There were things she needed to say to them.

Chapter XVI

She was at the cemetery by sunrise. Taking a seat on the curbing at the foot of the graves, she spat forth a barrage of thoughts and queries. She cried, she yelled, she cursed; she even threw small rocks at the headstones of her beloved grandparents, even though such actions bordered on heresy. And when she had spent herself emotionally, she sat quietly and waited for some insight, but none came. Because the uncertainty she was experiencing lay with Mama and Papa, she had hoped, but not expected, that being here would provide the clarity she needed so desperately. The living relatives, she prayed, would be more helpful.

When she arrived at Uncle Jack's, he and Aunt Laura Mae were just finishing breakfast and were surprised, but pleased, at such an early visit. Over a cup of coffee, she began her quest for explanations.

While he appeared sympathetic to her need to know, Uncle Jack offered little insight. As to why she hadn't known of Lynn's keeping track of her for years, he told her again of Zell's hatred of all things black and of the fear the family had experienced for themselves and others.

When she broached the issue of Mama and Miss Hattie's relationship, Aunt Laura Mae began quickly to clear the table while Uncle Jack blanched noticeably.

"I'm not sure I know what you're talkin' about," he finally offered after a long pause.

"Of course you do," Jane asserted more loudly than she had intended. "Lynn told me about their letters, phone calls, and friendship. Why, Uncle Jack?"

"They were both fine ladies, Jane Ellen; I reckon they just enjoyed each other's company and needed each other, even if it had to be by letters or the telephone instead of visitin' in one another's houses," Uncle Jack attempted to convince her.

"Bullshit!" she screamed, jumping from the table. Even before the word was out of her lips, she couldn't believe she had said that to her uncle and in her aunt's presence. Mama would have washed her mouth out with lye soap, but Mama wasn't here, and Jane wasn't sure what she would have done if her grandmother had been. More importantly, she wasn't sure she had known Mama as she thought she had.

Uncle Jack didn't flinch an inch at her outburst, and she continued. "You grew up in the segregated South just like I did, and you know open friendships didn't and still don't really exist between the two colors; everything is superficial. Now, the truth, please."

"Jane Ellen, I've told you all I can. Miss Hattie is the only one who can answer them questions you so intent on askin'," her uncle stated kindly, but firmly.

"She isn't doing well since Zell's death, and I hate to bother her. I don't understand why I have to chase the answers down. I am apparently the only one around her who doesn't know what went on, and continues to go on. Why couldn't I be trusted with this family secret, and how many other secrets are there?" Jane quizzed.

At that moment Aunt Laura Mae dropped a glass into the sink, creating an ear-shattering crash, and causing Jane to jump. It was a couple of seconds before Uncle Jack spoke again. "It wadn't no secret. It just wadn't that important, and still ain't. The two women was friends; that's all there was. They took comfort in talkin' and correspondin'. Miss Hattie was kind to us, always, but she was more so after Papa's death, and Mama appreciated it and let Miss Hattie know she did. They couldn't broadcast that for all the world to know for just the reasons you said. It was the South, and they was a lot of rules for folks to go by—still are, for that matter. The rules nowadays just don't hit you on the head as hard as they used to. You studyin' too much 'bout this, Chile. It really ain't nothin'"

"I don't believe you for a moment," Jane countered, "and I feel betrayed, by Mama particularly. It's as if she didn't respect and trust me enough to confide in me."

"Chile, nobody hadn't ever respected nobody more'n Mama respected you. She thought the sun rose and set in you. We all knowed she loved you better'n anybody 'cept Papa. But that was all right. She meant for you to get all the chances she never had, and she'd put anybody in they place that had any other ideas. That's the way it was from the time Papa died.

"You was her reason to go on. She meant you wouldn't ever need to depend on nobody, not a husband nor a white, nor anybody else, for nothin'. She realized after Papa died how much she had depended on him and then she had to jump right in dependin' on white folks. It wadn't that she resented it; she was just so independent minded. It had been her dream for herself to have some freedom, and she was so proud of you when you lived out that dream for her," Jack tried to explain.

All this Jane knew in her head, but her heart was affected by wounded pride, and she couldn't know what to think of the portion of her grandparents' lives she had been totally ignorant of.

She continued her interrogation, "Then why didn't she tell me about any of this? She didn't trust me, right?"

"Gracious, no! She just didn't know she needed to tell you. None of us did. It wadn't nothin' to tell. Miss Hattie was just helpin' out after Mr. Till killed Papa," Jack went on. "Miss Hattie felt guilty, and she hadn't had nothin' to do with it.

Mama knowed that and accepted her help, knowin' it was all the pore woman could do to make herself feel better."

"What about while Papa was still alive? Lynn says they knew each other even back then," Jane appealed.

"They did. Nothin' unusual 'bout that neither. Papa worked for Mr. Till; you know that," Jack detailed. "Miss Hattie tried to see 'bout us 'cause she knowed how Mr. Till was."

"That's another thing. Papa was intelligent. I thought he was the smartest man alive. Why did he work for Mr. Till? He was a horrible, evil man," Jane entreated.

"That's a fact, Baby," Jack smiled and stated, "about Mr. Till bein' horrible and evil and 'bout papa bein' smart, but what difference you think that made back then? He was still just another nigger to most folks, and niggers wadn't supposed to be smart. They was to work and keep they mouths shut. No, smartness didn't count for nothin'. In fact, I 'spect it was a bad thing. Too much thinkin' was a threat to the whites. But Papa knowed a job was a job, and the wages he made at the store was better'n most blacks was gettin' back then. Papa could put up with most things to make it easier for us. Miss Hattie seen 'bout him as much as she could, too."

"Uncle Jack, please tell me what Papa was accused of doing when Mr. Till shot him. Everybody thought I was too young to know at first, and then it was if nobody remembered any more when I got old enough to understand. I have tried for years to make some sense of it, but I can't. Papa was such a good man. I know that, even if I was young when he died. I can't imagine that he would ever deliberately do anything to hurt another person."

"You done explained it before, Jane Ellen. Mr. Till was a bad man. He didn't need no reason." Jane knew her uncle well enough to know his answer was evasive, but she was not to let him get by with such a sketchy reply. "What did Mr. Till give as the reason. He never spent a single minute in jail for the shooting. He must have made it sound as if Papa was guilty of something."

The exasperated man sighed before what was obviously a labored effort. When he spoke again, it was more slowly and with carefully chosen words. "He said Papa was messin' with Miss Hattie." He waited for Jane's reaction and continued only after no noticeable difference in her demeanor. "Some of the white folk that didn't know Papa jumped on that. Worst thing a black man could do was to mess with a white woman. Papa hadn't done nothin' but try to protect Miss Hattie from Mr. Till, but that fact never made it into some conversations. Didn't make it to the grand jury neither, which was natully all white men. Miss Hattie wadn't ever allowed to tell what she knew to be the truth. She wadn't even asked no questions by the law. She told Mama and me, though.

"Mr. Till was tryin' to beat her up again, in the storage room at the store. Papa walked in and got between them. Him and Mr. Till had words. That awful man walked to the front of the store, got the gun he kept under the counter, and shot Papa from behind. He fell dead at Miss Hattie's feet. She told us all this, Jane Ellen, but she didn't tell nobody else. She couldn't. Mr. Till would have killed her. I'm certain of it.

"That's why Miss Hattie tried, long as she could, to take care of y'all. Mama wouldn't let her any longer than she had to, though. She went to work with Miss Pat so she could try to make a living and not depend on Miss Hattie. I always will believe it was Miss Hattie paid Mama through Miss Pat all them years, but she never owned up to it. Last few years she ain't had much. Zell drunk up what little money they had saved, and the store business dried up. I go by and do odd jobs for her and Lynn when I can. Pie too. We don't have to sneak 'round like used to before Zell passed."

Jane allowed all the new information to soak in a bit before speaking. "Doesn't all this make you mad, Uncle Jack? Papa's name smeared all these years? That bastard getting away with murder? Miss Hattie not defending Papa to everybody?"

"At first, yeah," Jack admitted. "It would have eat me up if I hadda let it, but lots of innocent folks was killed and lots of names smeared in them days. It was just the way it was and we couldn't do nothin' about it, and Miss Hattie couldn't neither.

"Blacks that complained ended up dead theirselves, most times. Mama had seen lots of things I hadn't seen, and she understood how it was before I did. She kep' me from runnin' off at the mouth and gettin' killed myself. Kep' tellin' me she didn't intend to bury both her boys.

"Besides, Papa's name never really suffered. Wadn't many folks, white nor black, didn' know which of them two, Papa or Mr. Till, was the real man. Just couldn't nobody say it out loud. Lots of white folks helped us after Papa was gone. We just couldn't tell who they was. Just like lots of white folks helped get you elected sheriff but can't admit they did."

"I still don't understand if a number of whites knew Mr. Till was lying why the grand jury acted as it did. Surely, somebody had to speak out on Papa's behalf."

"Baby, you too young to remember how it was in them days. Didn't nobody much go agains' the system. Them that did was in danger of bein' done in by it. Couldn't none of them take the side of a black man against a white in public."

"I'm not sure I did the right thing in moving back here. I was so young and idealistic when I left the South and optimistic enough when I moved back to think we could all live together in harmony now. Without having to sneak around to do it. Apparently I was wrong, and I hate the fact. At least in New York people admit their coldness. They even have something of an arrogance about it. Here they keep it camouflaged behind the sweet smiles and false warmth. None of this is going to work, is it?" a deflated Jane pleaded.

Her uncle looked her squarely in the eyes as he declared, "Of course it is! Mama knew it. Even Papa knew it way back then. That's why we all had to get as much schoolin' as we possibly could. We had to be ready for it when it did come. That's why when you come along, you had to finish college. Mama hoped and prayed every day that it would get to where you could come back home and make a good livin' here. Wish she could have lived to see what you've done. It's because of people like you comin' home and good, smart people stayin' now that's gonna make the dream really come true for all of us. And you know this is better'n New York any day of the week. Up there wadn't just whites you couldn't have nothin' to do with. It was everybody. I done heard you complain too many times 'bout all that to believe you really think different."

"No," she admitted, "you're right. I do believe this is the best place in the world to live. But it's surely got a long way to go before it's right."

"Of course it does," Jack conceded, "but it's gettin' there. We're makin' more money than we ever dreamed of makin'. We're not scared all the time now. We can even walk into most businesses without lookin' over our shoulders. We can do most things 'cept go to church with the whites, and who wants that dead mess, anyhow?"

For the first time since the night before, Jane felt like laughing. Admittedly, she too cared nothing for the staid, somber services she had experienced the few times she had attended church with Sandra in the city. There were things about her culture she wanted to remain unchanged, without interference. She could give other cultures the same consideration. She was also thankful for the changes that had been made. She was sheriff, for goodness sake! She just felt helpless again, as she often had as a child, to right the wrongs that had been committed against her and her family. And she felt helpless to uncover the background she knew was hers.

She also felt guilty. She had vented all her frustrations on her dear, sweet Uncle Jack, so like Papa in his cool demeanor and patience. She, on the other hand, was like Mama, quick to anger and quick of tongue. Papa used to say Mama's tongue was connected in the middle so it could flap at both ends.

She rose to leave her uncle's house, ashamed and embarrassed. She grabbed her uncle and hugged him. "Please forgive me for unloading all my confusion and frustration on you. I'm truly sorry. I"ll try not to bother you with this again, but I'm going to see if I can learn more from anybody who'll tell me."

A forgiving uncle returned her embrace. "Honey, ain't no need apologizin'. You family. I know what it is to need answers you can't get, too, Just be careful what you ask and who you ask. I don't want you gettin' hurt over somethin' ain't worth worryin' with. Some things better not to go meddlin' with."

So there was really something she still didn't know. Uncle Jack's cryptic response verified it. What could it possibly be and how could she find out without disturbing poor old Miss Hattie who had obviously suffered enough already?

With no solid answers and little solace, Jane had, however, spent much of her wrath and frustration. The guilt still tugged at her, but she felt somewhat absolved of that, given Uncle Jack's forgiving nature. After such a jolt of emotions and with no food consumption since her feast with Lynn the previous night, she found herself ravenously hungry.

She drove to the only restaurant within fifteen miles, the Cafe in Bluff's Landing, where she grabbed a take-out burger and fries for herself and a burger for Abner. She drove home, shared the meal and a monologue about her morning with her four-footed companion, who was much more interested in the food, then took a long restful nap. When she finally stirred, the sun had set, and Abner was scratching at the back door to get out for his pre-bedtime bathroom break.

She checked with her office to make sure the deputies on duty truly were, let Abner back into the house, and settled down to a quiet night of senseless T.V. The kind she could watch without any thinking. It was hard to concentrate, and her mind wandered back to her conversation with Lynn that had begun this state of confusion in her. She was confident she didn't have enough information to decipher it all, and she had no idea about how to go about garnering that information.

She slept fitfully and experienced some of the most bewildering dreams of her life. She was in heaven, where she saw Papa and Mama and was just about ask them for an explanation when Zell appeared, head in hand. The mouth of the severed object was arranged in a permanent hideous grin whose stare was aimed directly at her, causing her to question her earlier assumption that she was in heaven.

If Zell was in the place, it most decidedly must be hell. But how could that be when Mama and Papa were here? She knew what saints her grandparents had been. She was crying out to them for help when Abner awakened her with his whining. Apparently she had been making audible sounds, not merely the silent screams of nightmares. She had to have answers. But how? Where? From whom?

Chapter XVII

The concerns of her job and those she had for Lynn necessarily took precedence over those for herself, and the need to know was relegated to the back burner, if only temporarily. The commissioners readily approved her request for the additional help, and Jane felt confident the decision was based partially, probably largely, on the fact that she had made it clear who the help would be. All the men knew she was accused of killing her husband, but obviously most of the residents knew of Lynn's prior and current problems and sympathized with her. This was, Jane figured, a good way for these men to salve their collective conscience for not having intervened earlier. That old Southern male code again, she told herself, but for once she was rather thankful for it. She certainly had no need to question their intent. She was much too excited about Lynn's working with her.

The minute the last commissioner left the room, she drove to Lynn with the news and the first batch of papers and explicit instruction for their completion. Lynn welcomed her into the kitchen where the poor woman who had begun life as a wealthy girl sobbed with joy over such a menial, low-paying job. Jane's own heart broke and burst with delight simultaneously. Lynn asked her to stay for a cup of coffee, but the room was too cold for human habitation, and she could look at Lynn and see her friend's exhaustion. Jane wished there was more she could do but knew that out-and-out charity was impossible.

These were proud people bred of proud people. In college sociology, she had learned that the section of Europe from which most Southern whites hailed originally—England, Scotland, and Ireland—was noted for hardy, warring peoples who held great regard for self preservation and familial ties. She had not given that knowledge much thought at the time her professor presented it. Now she remembered it and watched it carried out lo these many years later in its saddest rendering.

Pride could be such a deadly force, but she respected it in others just as she recognized its importance in her own life as well as in the lives of her family members before her. So she politely refused the coffee, in what she hoped and prayed was a blithe manner, walked briskly to her car where she cried uncontrollably all the way home.

Not a day passed now without her checking on Lynn and asking about the yet unseen Miss Hattie. Pie was her source of information on days when even a short visit would not fit into her harried schedule. Because of her earlier mistrust and what bordered on hatred for someone she now realized had been a victim of the same system as she, part of her concern for Miss Hattie was the result of guilt. She could not verbalize that to anyone, not even Lynn, but she knew in her heart that it was a fact.

Each Friday afternoon she retrieved Lynn's work and sometimes sat a moment for a visit and a cup of coffee in the kitchen. Never any farther in the house and never did she see Miss Hattie. She did detect a noticeable warming in the room after the first couple of weeks. About the same time, she also tasted the fact that the coffee was obviously a better brand than that first weak cup weeks earlier before Lynn's paychecks from the county began arriving. The best improvement, however, was in Lynn's attitude and appearance. There was more color in her cheeks, and the curves were reappearing, if only slightly. The salary was making its mark just as Jane believed it might, prayed it would.

After her second paycheck, Lynn had the phone reconnected, and the two old friends began a new ritual. On every night, except Friday when they visited in person, they talked. The conversations were usually brief and inconsequential, but Jane relished them and knew by the upbeat tone of Lynn's voice that she did, too. Miss Hattie and her condition were always discussed, and according to Lynn the older lady grew better each day but was still extremely depressed. She never left the house and seldom ventured out of her room. Jane prayed Lynn did not shoulder the blame in the eyes of Zell's mother. From her own abbreviated stint at maternity, she recognized it as a powerful force.

Neither the events leading up to the fateful night nor the night itself was ever spoken of by either of the women since their first conversation after Zell's funeral. That is until the week before the grand jury was to meet, in early March. On a Friday afternoon, over a glass of iced tea, Jane explained to Lynn the procedure. She had never asked, and while Jane had thought that odd, she had never mentioned it either. Now it had to be done. When Lynn learned that there would be no testimony, just the state's presentation of the facts, she burst into tears,

"You mean neither Miss Hattie nor I will have to say anything?" she sobbed.

"Neither of you will even be there." Jane explained. "I'll show the pictures of both you and the body as well as the condition of the house, particularly your bedroom. Doc Jones and Seth will also probably tell what they observed. Besides, as we've discussed before, the media has already made most of this an exercise in futility. Everybody there will have seen all the evidence before. It shouldn't take but a few minutes, and I feel really good about it. You know how the people in this county feel about you, and they all knew what was going on, if they didn't step in to help."

"Nobody expected anybody to help. That's just the way it was. I'm not sorry he's dead, though. I'm just sorry Miss Hattie is suffering so because of it. He's caused her such pain, both while he was alive and now after he's dead. I've tried to reason with her, but she acts as if she doesn't hear me. I can't get through the emotional wall. It's not like she didn't know how mean he was. I don't think he was capable of loving, no matter how hard she tried to teach him. Mr. Till taught him to hate, and he learned that lesson well. A part of her has to be relieved, too, but she won't admit it. Can't admit it," Lynn said.

Again Jane found herself surprised by this revelation. "I thought it was just blacks he hated. I had no idea it was everybody."

"Blacks were away up the list of what he despised in the world, but he distrusted or detested everything. I watched as Miss Hattie spent her life trying to show him some of the positive things and people, even tried myself at first, but he wouldn't think of letting down his guard. If he started trusting her, me, or anything else, he acted like he thought something would jump up and get him. So, he just kept right on hating and lashing out, up to the end. Miss Hattie will be so relieved she doesn't have to say anything at the hearing, though. That is the main thing she has been so worried about, although she worried about my testifying, too."

Jane chose her next words carefully. "I have thought so often about the mother of a gunshot victim and the person who pulled the trigger living in the same house, and I'm not sure I think it's a good idea, no matter how understanding the mother may be. Are you certain you and she need to continue your present arrangement? It must be awkward for both of you."

Lynn, however, took no time to ponder her own response. "Nonsense! We both are aware of what's happened, obviously, but neither of us has any ill will. I wouldn't dream of living apart from her, nor would she ever choose to live away from me. Maybe it's strange, but we truly still love each other as mother and daughter."

Jane shook her head. "I'm happy for you, if you're convinced that's the case."

"Of course I'm sure," Lynn assured her.

Again Jane thought carefully about her words before continuing. "I've got to ask you a few things about that night, too. Did you feel your life was threatened?"

This time Lynn also thought for a moment before answering. She stared at a scar on the back of her right hand when she did speak. "Yes. Each time he hit me, I knew he was capable of killing me. He would get so worked up and completely lose control. He was so strong when that happened, and toward the end, it happened often. From the first time he hit me, I believed he could kill me whenever he chose, with his bare hands. And figured he would some day."

Jane tried to distance herself emotionally as she attempted to proceed as she would have done with John Q. Public, if John Q. Public had apparently killed someone as a defense move. "This was not the first time something like that had happened, then?"

"Certainly not. It was a regular occurrence for him to be mad with someone about something and lash out at Miss Hattie or me or both."

Again, Jane tried to treat this as any other routine case. "Why then did you choose that night to defend yourself?" Then she added to her friend, "Lynn, I have to know before I go before the grand jury."

Lynn began to clear away the empty cups and to wipe the counter top anxiously. This was a hideous scene to have to replay, Jane realized, but the emotion she observed in Lynn was stark terror. It was in her eyes. In order to present the case convincingly Jane needed to know, but she realized from past professional experience that Lynn had probably revealed all she was going to about that night—at least now. She was a private person, Jane rationalized, and there was that pride thing again. She would just have to convince the grand jury without really knowing what triggered the violence she could never fathom in her friend. It wouldn't be an issue, she thought; Lord, she hoped.

The day of the hearing, Jane threw up immediately upon arising and could not stomach even a cup of coffee. She prayed her stomach wouldn't growl during the proceedings. It didn't.

Everything went exactly as she had expected. The eighteen members of the grand jury (three white males, five black females, six white females, and four black males) had their decision made long before they arrived, and any other combination of male, female, black, white in the county would have done the same. The story of what had happened that night had circulated back and forth in every social and economic level in the area, and there was nobody who felt Lynn should be punished any more that she already had been during her marriage.

A "no bill" decision was rendered, and Jane made no pretense of decorum. She broke from the courtroom to her office to call Lynn. When she revealed the verdict, the gasp from the other end of the line, followed by the crying, were the sounds she had waited to hear. It was really over now, and they both could get on with their lives, particularly Lynn. She thanked Jane profusely but asked to cut the conversation short so she could relay the good news to Miss Hattie. As she hung up, Jane marveled at the truly unique relationship the two Mrs. Greens shared.

Chapter XVIII

The next Friday when Jane went by to exchange the work papers, she was surprised at how much better Lynn looked. She had talked to her daily, by phone, but hadn't seen her since the grand jury's ruling. All the waiting and wondering had been a bigger strain than she had thought. Lynn actually initiated conversation and laughed quite often. She had dressed more carefully, too, and had taken the time to apply makeup. Jane thought she looked quite pretty and told her so. That brought a blush and an apology.

"I felt a little guilty fixing up. It's as if I'm celebrating Zell's death. But I can't remember when I've felt so free and relieved. Miss Hattie insisted on it. She said I had sat in sack cloth and ashes long enough."

"I agree wholeheartedly," Jane said. "Miss Hattie is a wise woman. Listen to her. Speaking of which, how is she?"

"Much better," Lynn gushed." She is even making plans to attend church Sunday. She just dreads seeing everybody again for the first time. She hasn't been out since the funeral. She thinks people will be talking about her. I've tried to assure her that she's old news. They've got a new carcass to pick by this time. I hope she won't relent and refuse to go. She needs to get out."

"Certainly. Besides, just because Zell was her son doesn't make her guilty of anything. She has no reason to be embarrassed. On a selfish note," Jane continued, "do you think she might feel like talking to me now? I feel so estranged from my own family because I don't know so many things that obviously went on. I especially feel estranged from Mama and Papa. I'm not sure I really knew them."

"Don't be silly! Of course you knew them. They were two of the finest people who ever walked! They were exactly who you knew them to be."

"How can you be so sure?" Jane probed. "You didn't even know Papa. He died before you and I met."

"I feel as if I knew him. Miss Hattie has told me all about both of them, especially of their younger days," Lynn told her.

"Well, I guess that means you know more than I do," an exasperated Jane sighed. "I know very little about their childhoods, particularly Papa's. He died so young, and I don't guess Mama kept in close contact with his family. I never knew any of them. Will you tell me what you know?"

Lynn sat facing her friend and looked at her kindly and squarely in the eyes. "Be patient and try to wait for Miss Hattie, until she feels better. If she can pull herself together, I know she would want to be the one to answer all your questions. She and your grandparents were contemporaries; so she knows more, anyway."

"Cryptic answers again. Was there an axe murderer somewhere in my not-too-distant heritage?" Jane half joked, half pleaded.

"On the contrary, Jane; they were fine, upstanding people just as you think they were," Lynn assured her. "You're worrying too much about this. I wish I had never mentioned the friendship between them and Miss Hattie. You have been overanalyzing everything since then."

No use in expending unnecessary time concerning herself with things she could not change, Jane decided. She dropped the subject—at least for the moment.

As the sheriff of such a poor, rural county she had enough to occupy her mind with other matters. The population of approximately 7,000 citizens, largely black, was sparsely spread over about 950 square miles. The county seat of Parksville boasted 875, give or take a few. Bluff's Landing, four and a half miles to the north, claimed 327, but the count was probably somewhat lower, and Fultonville, six miles south of Parksville, had somewhere around 550.

There were a number of other wide places in the road with community names, but those were the only incorporated towns containing the only three post offices. Most of the people lived in the countryside, making her job and that of her staff more difficult.

There were robberies, murders, rapes, domestic violence, and all the other crimes of the big city, merely on a smaller scale. Drunk men beat their women here just as they had in Harlem, angry women stabbed or shot their men just as they had in New York, lazy people stole things exactly as they had in the streets, and stupid, misguided children here also did stupid, misguided deeds just as they had in her past experience. Here she often had to drive miles and miles to do something about any of it.

Now, just as in her past, it was the youth who troubled her most. So, just as she had done earlier, she did all she could to improve conditions for the young, impressionable ones who could make the positive changes in the future in this region she adored.

She began a one-woman campaign—recruiting everyone who would listen and give her even an ounce of encouragement. Ministers, judges, lawyers, fellow police officers from her staff and surrounding areas, white businessmen and their black counterparts, housewives, laborers, educators, and the youth themselves were recruited heavily. She didn't know if she could make a difference, but she'd damned sure be caught trying.

Workdays were long, followed by meetings with others who wanted to effect a change. Most nights she collapsed into bed, with little energy for anything except her latest crusade.

She and Lynn had their same working relationship as well as their personal one. They visited when they could, talked on the phone almost daily, and exchanged papers and pleasantries over a cup of coffee or a glass of iced tea each Friday. The arrangement established when Lynn first started working with the sheriff's department was exactly as it had been at first. So, on a Friday in June, it came as quite a shock to Jane when it was Miss Hattie, not Lynn who met her at the kitchen door and welcomed her into the house.

Another shocking aspect was Miss Hattie's physical appearance. She looked perky, for lack of a better word. She was trim and appeared fit, with her attire and makeup impeccable, just as Jane remembered it from her own youth. The woman had been getting out more and more frequently, according to Lynn's reports, but Jane had not seen her, until now, since from the back seat of the limousine on the day of Zell's funeral.

The older woman held the door open and embraced the younger as if she were a long lost, dear friend. Jane did not quite know how to respond. She certainly respected Miss Hattie, particularly since she had heard all Lynn and Uncle Jack had revealed, but she wasn't prepared for such a warm greeting. She returned the embrace, but she feared with mush less enthusiasm than that of her hostess. There was still, she hated to admit, the fact of Papa's death. She regained her composure, she hoped, before Miss Hattie noted the hesitation.

Apparently she hadn't noticed; for she proceeded with a verbal welcome. "Jane Ellen, I'm so happy to see you at last. It's been too long. I'm so sorry to have kept you at bay. I just wasn't emotionally fit to deal with your professional questions earlier."

"Miss Hattie, I understand completely. You have had every right to your privacy and time to heal. I am so sorry about your loss and the circumstances surrounding it." Jane heard her own words and couldn't believe that she was speaking them and couldn't believe that she actually meant them.

"Jane Ellen, that is very kind of you," Miss Hattie sighed. "I know that my family has caused you so much grief. I only hope I can make it up to you as much as is possible in the short time I have left. I know nobody can replace all that you've lost, but there are some things I believe I can do to make it easier for you. Please say you'll give me a chance to try."

"More cryptic messages," Jane mused silently. Aloud she stated, "Don't worry about making anything up to me. You don't owe me anything, and actually I'm quite happy now. I never thought I would be able to say any of that to someone whose last name is 'Green,' but with a lot of soul searching and so many years, I've thankfully reached that point. I have to be honest, Miss Hattie, and tell you that I'm glad it's you and not one of the male members of your family I'm having this conversation with. I seriously doubt that I could have been so magnanimous with Zell or Mr. Till. I hope someday I can forgive all of it."

The two women had seated themselves at the kitchen table facing each other. Miss Hattie looked directly at Jane and spoke. "I of all people understand the anger and hatred you must feel for Zell and Till. I am delighted to know that you don't harbor similar hatred for me. I have worried so long and have agonized over your negative feelings. Even as a very young girl you didn't hold me in such high regard, and that pained me more than you could possibly know. I understood how you felt even then, though."

A repentant Jane reached across the table and placed her hand on top of the thin, pale hand of her hostess. "I asked Lynn to express to you my regrets about my earlier mistrust of you. That was wrong of me. I realize now that none of the hurt I bore was your fault. It was just such a great loss for me when Papa died, and I hated everything and everybody I felt was even remotely responsible, including you. Then Zell terrorized me, and I allowed the hate and fear to fester and grow."

Miss Hattie released an audible gasp as she allowed Jane's last statement to sink in. After a brief moment, a tear dripped down her right cheek and she spoke again. "I suspected him of evil that day out at your house when we delivered the supplies. I even accused him, but as always he denied it. He had that hideous smirk on his face he always displayed when he had been especially offensive. I guess I really didn't want to know. I didn't pursue it. That was when it was, wasn't it?"

Now it was Jane's turn to let fall a tear, followed by an audible whimper born of anger, fear, regret, sadness, and release. Finally, she composed herself enough to respond. "Yes, ma'am, it was. He said things I couldn't interpret then, and later when I finally did understand their meaning, I didn't understand. Why was he angry enough to hurl them at me? I was afraid to tell anybody. I was scared people would think I had done something wrong. Even Mama never knew."

With that revelation, Jane's tears flowed as they hadn't in years over that aspect of her life. Miss Hattie retrieved a box of tissues and allowed her to vent her emotions before the older woman spoke again. "I am so sorry! No wonder you hated us so. I'm not sure I could be so forgiving, as you seem to be. I rationalized that I couldn't have prevented your pain, but I should have done something about Zell's treatment of you. I knew, but wouldn't admit, he had committed a wrong. I wouldn't allow myself to imagine what it was. He didn't hurt you physically, did he?"

Jane knew this had probably been a question the woman had been afraid to ask but one which she had to have answered at this point. She was relieved that she could honestly give her the answer she had waited so long to hear.

"No, m'aam. He never touched me. Mama walked back into the kitchen. Besides, I had a knife that I intended to use to prevent him from doing anything of the kind. Maybe if he had come toward me I could have prevented all the pain and agony his living caused you and Lynn later. I almost wish he had given me the opportunity."

"Oh, no, child, that would have been too much of a burden for you to carry at such a young age," Miss Hattie assured her. "I'm sorry Zell had to die as he did, but I'm thankful that you haven't had to deal with the guilt of committing the act yourself."

Jane thought this was a unique sentiment, given the fact that her daughter-in-law, the one she professed to care about greatly, instead had the dubious honor of shouldering that burden. She kept the opinion to herself.

It was Miss Hattie who spoke next. "It appears to me that you have used the negative events of your early childhood in a positive way. Because you were angry and frustrated with the system, you have spent a lifetime trying to change it, and most effectively, I might add. That must be of little consolation to you, but I would say that much of your compassion for people is probably a direct result of the trauma of that time. You have used it as a springboard for improvement. That is a portion of the rationalization of many years of pondering over my part in it all, I know. I had to have some way to ease some of my distress, given my contribution, the fact that I didn't stop any of it."

Jane rose from her chair, walked around the table, and placed her hands on Miss Hattie's shoulders, resting her head on top of that of the old lady, who was sobbing uncontrollably. "I really don't blame you at all. We were all victims of the system that said we had no choices, no control, in our lives. I hated Mr. Till and Zell. I still do. I pray someday to turn that loose, but I'm not capable yet. But I feel no hatred toward you. Not now. As far as I'm concerned, you had nothing to do with any of it, and you have nothing to feel guilty about nor do you have anything to make up to me."

Miss Hattie rose, embraced Jane, buried her head on the sheriff's shoulder, and cried the tears of an emancipated prisoner. When she finally regained a semblance of composure, she held Jane at arm's length as she said, "I hope you will always feel that way. It is important to me that you and I become friends, if that is possible."

With that she left the kitchen, and Lynn entered to a most confused Jane. Apparently aware of at least the general content of the conversation just completed, she smiled at her friend and said, "I'm glad she finally felt comfortable talking to you. She's been wanting to for weeks but couldn't muster the courage until now. She didn't know what your reaction would be and feared your rejection. She looked pleased just now when I met her in the hall. Must have gone all right."

"I guess. I'm still not quite sure what it was she meant to accomplish," Jane admitted. "She took me by complete surprise. She didn't make small talk before getting down to the crux of the matter. She has been stewing over this for a while, hasn't she? Another thing that surprised me is how good she looks."

"Yes," Lynn verified. "She has been stewing over it for years. Your opinion of her is of utmost importance, and she knows at her age she couldn't have long to live. She doesn't feel she has time for small talk. As far as her appearance is concerned, she has been a different person since the grand jury's decision. She was really worried about me. I'm not sure she could have endured losing me. She has lost everything she has ever loved before. When the verdict was rendered, she began immediately to improve physically and emotionally. She really does look good, doesn't she? I hope and pray she can have peace and quiet for the rest of her days. Nobody deserves it more."

"Was that a subtle way of telling me I don't need to trouble her with my endless barrage of questions about hers and my grandparents' relationship?"

"Oh, no, I didn't mean that at all!" Lynn assured her. "I think she will be glad to tell you anything you want to know now that she is confident you have no ill feelings toward her. I do have one request, though. Let her do it at her convenience and in her own way. Don't pressure her."

"Certainly, Jane promised. "I've waited this long; I can surely wait a while longer. And now, if you don't mind, I'm going home. I have a number of emotions I need to sort through."

With a speedy retreat, she returned to her cottage to mull over the latest turn of events. The next day, Saturday, was a day off, and she intended to spend it doing nothing, with Abner, while she ruminated more about her rather strange meeting the night before. Instead, at 7:05 in the morning, the phone roused her. It was Lynn.

"Sorry to bother you so early, Jane," she apologized. I know how little rest you've been getting lately, but Miss Hattie insisted I call you. Will you and Abner join us for breakfast? Miss Hattie wants to talk to you."

How could she refuse, exhausted though she was. This was what she had been waiting for so long. She dressed hurriedly, talking to Abner all the while, advising him of the joint breakfast invitation. He wagged his tail as if he understood, but she figured it was her tone rather than the words he appreciated.

Chapter XIX

When she approached the screen door of the now familiar kitchen, the delicious aromas met her. There was coffee, ham, and biscuits she recognized immediately, and others she couldn't distinguish yet. She smiled as she recalled the pitiful gravy and biscuits of her earlier visits. And that awful coffee!

Miss Hattie again met her at the door and again embraced her warmly. This time Jane was able to return the gesture sincerely. Lynn turned from her spot in front of the stove and extended her own welcome to her friend and to her friend's dog, whose tail had been in perpetual motion since arriving.

The smells from the interior were even better than from the porch, and Jane found herself involuntarily salivating. Her busy schedule left little time for the morning meal on workdays, and she seldom bothered on her days off. She hadn't realized how much she missed the rite until that minute.

Lynn was just taking the biscuits out of the oven and asked Jane to pour the coffee while she prepared Abner a special plate of biscuits drizzled with ham gravy. She set it beside the stove for the eager canine.

The three ladies sat down to the table set with the good china, damask napkins, and sterling flatware. While eating, they discussed the weather, politics, Jane's crusade for the county's youth, and the local gardening situation. Nothing any more serious. However, as soon as the last bit of jelly had been devoured on the last crumb of biscuit, Miss Hattie invited Jane to come with her. Following her down the hall, Jane went with the older lady into the same room she had found in such disarray the only other time she had entered this part of the house.

Standing just inside the doorway, Jane watched Miss Hattie walk to an old trunk in one corner of the room and retrieve a large, black photo album. Carrying the parcel to the bed, she sat, motioning for Jane to join her. Placing the leather-bound album in Jane's lap, she invited her to open it and look through.

"This is something I should have shared with you long ago. I never meant to keep it a secret. It's just that things kept happening to weaken my resolve," Miss Hattie quietly stated.

Jane slowly turned the decaying pages of the collection of pictures of people of very obvious wealth. Their clothing and surroundings were quite opulent. She had no idea why she was going through this apparent family album until on the fifth opening she spotted a picture that stopped her blood in its circuit.

Standing under a large oak tree in a light linen suit was Papa, but it wasn't Papa either. It was a white Papa, but not a white Papa either. The man in the photo must have been born a good twenty, maybe thirty, years before her grandfather, but there was the same frame, the same ramrod posture, and the same unmistakable crooked smile.

Miss Hattie noted the object of her attention and her bewilderment and answered her question before she could voice it. "That is a picture of my father as a young man. Cut quite a dashing figure, didn't he? He was always so handsome."

No response from Jane. The statement had merely served to muddle things more. She finally composed herself enough to form a verbal thought. "Miss Hattie, you must recognize that he looks just like Papa. In fact, that's exactly as I remember Papa, with the exception, of course, of the light skin. Why, I even know that hat your father is wearing. Mama kept it in the chifferobe in their room. What does this man have to do with Papa?"

"That man, my father, was his father, too," she said, watching Jane closely for her reaction.

"This white man was Papa's daddy? Papa was your brother?" she barely managed to squeak out the words, feeling her air passages close as she feared she was about to faint.

Noting her shock but confident that she would be all right, Miss Hattie continued. "Half brother. We had different mothers. Your great grandmother, Stump's mother, was our cook when I was a child, but she was much more than that. Both her parents had died in the terrible flu epidemic that killed so many people. Entire families were wiped out in many instances.

"Because her family had always worked for our family, even before the abolition of slavery, there was a moral obligation to take her in. Even if that had not been the case, I'm sure my mother would have welcomed her with open arms. She was a child who desperately needed a mother, and Mama was happy to oblige.

"Mama's own pregnancy while carrying me had been very difficult, and her doctor warned her never to try again. I was her only child and would always be. My mother saw to that, but she had maternal instincts she needed to put to use.

"The toddler's appearance at our house gave vent to some of those instincts. Missy's room was next to mine, and though she was black and I was white, we were sisters in every way but blood.

"I was three when she moved in as a two-year-old, and I don't remember there being any difference in the way we were treated by Mama, but Papa always was distant with her. I recall wondering why he didn't take her into his lap as he did me. I'm sure she must have wondered, too, or maybe she instinctively understood how it was; I don't know."

Again Miss Hattie paused to check the reaction of her captive one-woman audience. Jane stared at her with rapt attention but appeared capable of listening to more of the untangling of her forebears' twisted background.

Miss Hattie, therefore, continued. "At any rate, when time came for Missy to go to school, Mama refused to send her. In most instances, Papa had the last word, but this was one time when Mama stood her ground. He thought she had to go, for appearances. But Mama knew the schools for blacks were substandard. Remember how bad you thought they were? Your grandmother told me how awful Miss Cain was to you. Imagine education so soon after the Civil War when many people still believed blacks were possessions, incapable and unworthy of education.

"Mama didn't want that for our Missy. She taught her at home and taught her well. Because they were home alone together while I was in school, it was natural that Missy learn to emulate Mama in the kitchen. She was a quick study at it, as she was at everything she tried. It wasn't long before she became more proficient than Mama and took over the cooking duties, primarily. That suited Papa just fine. It was good for appearances. The little pickaninny had an acceptable reason to live in the house now; a lot of wealthy people had live-in help, and Mama had a full-time cook, another status symbol.

"Mama never viewed hers and Missy's relationship that way, though. They were a mother-daughter duo, and their banter in the kitchen while I studied often irritated me no end. In spite of my desire not to be, and my constant reassurance to myself that there was no reason to be, I was jealous of their common territory, the kitchen, and the extensive time they spent together each day without me. Sometimes I would find myself being mean to Missy without intending to be but almost without being able to stop myself. She never returned my spiteful attitude. She just loved me more and tried to make me happy any way she could."

Jane had not moved an inch from her position on the bed as Miss Hattie's story unraveled. She showed no emotion but exhibited rapt attention as the saga continued.

"When she got pregnant, she was only fourteen. Mama knew it immediately, even before Missy understood it. I never realized it was possible for a human being to be as hurt as my mother was. Not because Papa had broken their wedding vows, but that he had done so with her daughter. She never came close to forgiving him, but she never forgave herself either. Maybe if she hadn't shut him out so many nights in her paranoid attempt to prevent her own pregnancy, perhaps he would not have ravished Missy. I think it was probably inevitable, given his thinking toward blacks. He had to make Missy submissive in some way, and that was the only way he could figure to do it. I wondered, later, when I was old enough to wonder about such things, if Missy might have felt that his advances were her father's way of finally paying some attention to her.

"Whatever the thinking and the background cause, at fourteen years and eleven months, poor little Missy, my playmate up to and including the day she delivered, gave birth in her bedroom still decorated with dolls and tea sets. The healthy baby boy, even then, looked exactly like Papa. Our family doctor delivered him and did his best for Missy, but Stump was a big baby, and little Missy was tiny. Obstetrics bordered on butchery, then, too, and Missy died that night trying to nurse her hungry son.

"I was wracked with guilt for my jealousy of her and angrier than I believed possible toward my father. Mama's maternal instincts revved up again as she cared for Stump like he too was her own. Papa sank deeper and deeper into the bottle he had come to rely on heavily since Missy first got pregnant, and I determined not to make the mistake of being jealous of Stump as I had of poor Missy.

"You know, of course, that his name most assuredly was not "Stump" in our household. It was James Amos, after Mama's father and her father's father. Papa gave him his lifelong nickname after he quit using his left hand completely at about five. He was naturally left-handed, and Papa couldn't abide that since he was also left-handed as were both his brothers and their father. The black baby's hand preference was a constant reminder of his paternity and a threat to what my father believed to be his well kept secret.

"Of course there weren't ten people who didn't know the story. Missy had not been exposed to any other people, for God's sake. At any rate, Papa's drunken reasoning prompted him to prevent the baby's using his left hand by tying it behind his back with a belt until the appendage became virtually useless. This was the only interference Mama allowed Papa, but she didn't fight him on that. Perhaps there was a part of her that wanted to purge them of the proof positive of his abominable act. Whatever their thinking, James Amos Steiner became "Stump" when his hand first began hanging worthlessly at his side as it did for the remainder of his life."

For the first time since Miss Hattie began her monologue, Jane almost whispered to herself more than aloud to Miss Hattie, "Just like Zell."

"What, Honey?" Miss Hattie inquired.

"Papa was left-handed, just like Zell. I remember thinking Zell's hand preference must be straight from hell, just like he was, but that couldn't be the case if he shared those genes with Papa. There was not an evil thing about Papa," Jane reasoned aloud to herself.

Miss Hattie reaffirmed her. "You're absolutely right, dear. He was perhaps the gentlest creature I ever knew, just like his mother. But remember when he'd get excited and would stammer in search of just the right word? That's a trait often found in left-handed males; all the males in my father's family exhibited it. George Bush was left-handed and manifested it. During his presidential administration, a great deal was written on the subject. I read every word."

As more and more of the implications of all of Miss Hattie's disclosure sank in, Jane wondered who else was privy to the knowledge. "Does Lynn know all this?" she asked.

"Yes," she was advised. "As soon as I discovered what a truly lovely girl she was, I confided in her. I had to have somebody to help me sneak around. She was a brave soul, inviting further abuse because of it, but she never once questioned my telling her. She loved you and your family so much, she would have done anything to help."

Peeling one layer at a time off the mystery that was her heritage and attempting to determine the extent to which those around her had known, she inquired about the other family of her youth. "Did Lynn's parents know?"

"Of course. I'm telling you everyone of that era knew without being told, but I shared with them the whole sordid story," Miss Hattie confessed. "I had to have help after Stump died. At first I could slip around and get things to ya'll, but then Macy declared her independence and refused what she termed 'charity.' I thought it was just family taking care of family. Then too, Zell became so incensed by my actions and reported all my deeds to his father. It became an impossible situation.

"I went to Pat, Lynn's mother, and told her I would pay Macy if she could work in the Wambles household. Naturally Pat and George refused my money but hired her anyway, paying her what was an excellent salary for that era. When their fortunes vanished, there was no way to duplicate the sham. Besides, Macy was older and tired by that time. Retirement was the acceptable course of action."

Still grasping for the full impact of this knowledge newly acquired, she was yet curious as to who knew of it during its onset. "Mr. Till knew the whole story all the time, too?"

"Yes. In the beginning of our courtship, he gave me the impression that he was truly understanding," the old woman shared. "He wanted to know the minute details, which I told him. He used it later to hurt me and to separate my child from me. But, he had heard it all before my telling him. Ours was probably the only household in the county where it wasn't discussed, but the circumstances made me unfit for any of the fine young gentlemen around, according to the moral code of the day.

"I went off to college after high school, as I was reared to do, leaving Mama, Papa, and Stump at home. Your grandfather was only two when I left, and I had a much harder time telling him goodbye than I did either of my parents. Of course, by that time I hated my father, but I still adored Mama. Stump was my heart, though. Because I was so much older, I had been allowed a very active part in his day-to-day care.

"I understood what a stigma having acknowledged black kin was, and though I dated a bit in college, I didn't dare bring anybody from school home with me. Oh, mind you, a lot of the prominent men around had babies with the black help or with some of the pretty young back girls in the quarters, but the men didn't acknowledge the paternity except to their contemporaries when their tongues were loosened by the expensive brandy or the cheap homemade stuff they drank with equal relish. Those were strange times, Jane Ellen. You can't imagine the mores of that day, but they were ingrained in everybody, even the ones of us who knew the system was wrong."

"So how did you and Mr. Till get together, Miss Hattie?"

"When I graduated college and came home with a liberal arts degree, I had nothing productive to do. I puttered around the house helping Mama and resuming care of my little brother. Like Missy, he wasn't allowed to attend the substandard black schools. I got to teach him, and what a privilege it was! He was so eager to learn and so smart! I taught him everything I could remember from every course I had taken.

"He could read beautifully, and not just Spot and Pug, but also the classics—Shakespeare, Poe, Dickinson, Milton, and Chaucer. He was also tutored in music, etiquette, dress, art, and the Bible. Mama insisted on the Bible. When life became so warped and took so many strange turns for her, Mama turned more and more to the Bible and to God for answers, and she made sure Stump and I did, too.

"We all went to church regularly—Mama and I to the white Baptist congregation, and first Missy then Stump to the black A.M.E. church. Because our services ended earlier, we alternately froze and melted waiting in the car each Sunday until the black minister pronounced the benediction. Papa often fussed when Sunday dinner was late, but that didn't stop Mama. We were going to get our spiritual training, regardless.

"But Stump loved the literature of the Bible as much as its spiritual implications. I have never heard the most gifted preachers read it with such eloquence and gorgeous elocution as did my brother."

"Oh, I know!" Jane exclaimed. "The happiest times of my childhood were the hours Papa and I spent in his straight-back chair with him reading to me from his Bible—now my Bible. It's still my most prized possession."

"Mama gave him that when he learned all the books from Genesis to Revelation. It was his most prized possession, too, even as a young lad," Miss Hattie boasted.

"Of course. I had no idea. He said it was a gift from his mother. He considered her his mother," Jane again did her reasoning aloud.

"She was the only mother he ever knew," Miss Hattie continued to reveal. "He was told early on about Missy, but Mama was the nurturing force, and I did my part, too. Papa tried not to look at his son and never devoted any time to him. Of course, by the time I returned from college, Papa devoted little time to any of us. He went to the store early each morning Monday through Saturday, worked until after dark, ate supper in his room before drinking himself to sleep. I remember liking it that way, though. Mama, Stump, and I had our own little family circle that excluded Papa, and that was fine by me.

"When Stump was only fourteen, he went to work full-time in the store. Mama was bitterly opposed, but Papa was no longer able, because of his excessive drinking, to handle the responsibility. He was often too sick to get up and go to work; so he would send Stump instead.

"He was so much more efficient than Papa had been for years that the business prospered like it had never done. Because a successful white establishment could not possibly be turned over exclusively to a black, albeit half black son of the proprietor, I was also sent along to pretend I was in charge. I greeted the customers and tried to act as if Stump was the hired hand, but I knew nothing about the store business and cared even less. Nobody was fooled. I knew everybody else knew, and I didn't care about that either. I would have announced it from the rooftop except for Mama. She was still embarrassed by it all. Not the fact that Stump was a member of the family, but the fact that Papa had committed such an evil deed.

"So, I was an 'old maid' storekeeper when Till Green started coming around. I was flattered by his attention when he would come into the store, and I was not receiving too many other offers. Remember, I wasn't marriage material to the elitist families. Till's family had had money and land but had lost most of it because of poor management. He was still trying to keep up the charade and maintain the family farm, but the acreage had dwindled to the point of being below subsistence means of income.

"I should have known he was just trying to get his hands on Papa's estate, but I saw what I wanted to see. My biological clock was ticking, as you young folks would say, and I wanted a child I could love as I had loved baby Stump. Besides, I was damaged goods, and that didn't seem to bother Till. Your Papa didn't trust him from the beginning but said little. Even with his sheltered raising, he understood his place.

"I was thirty-two when Till and I married and moved in with Mama, Papa, and Stump. Till claimed it was just until he could build a nice new house of our own. He even had me laying out the design I wanted. But he never had any intention of doing anything but waiting for my parents to die.

"Stump married Macy the next year, and Papa gave them the eight acres of land where the two houses are now. Don't you think that was generous? Papa owned twelve hundred acres of rich pasture land handed down from his family, and he gave his only son eight acres he won off a drunk sharecropper's son in a poker game. The good inheritance was reserved for me, the white child -even a daughter. For all appearances, I was the only child.

"Stump never complained, though. I think he was surprised and grateful to get that. He had been raised to expect nothing from Papa. The old drunk was so happy to have his black child out of the house and out of sight that he must have had a temporary mental lapse and moment of generosity. Mama probably had something to do with it, too.

"Mama was devastated over Stump's marriage, however. Her baby was leaving home much too soon. She loved Macy but wasn't sure she was good enough. She was not educated, like Stump. In fact, she had never been allowed to attend school, starting to work in a white man's kitchen as a child. She was such a dear soul, and Mama had been resigned to his liking her after they met at church, but she thought it was just puppy love until at seventeen he announced they were already married. Blacks often married at extremely young ages during those times. That way they could reproduce and provide more cheap labor. Actually, by some standards, Stump was rather old at the time of his marriage.

"At any rate, the newly-weds lived with Macy's folks until they could build a house of their own. Believe it or not, Papa provided their home. He even had his hired hands build it. It was a really good house by black standards of the day, but it was far from what Stump had been accustomed to. He was master of his household, however, and he took to the role well. He was only eighteen when Macy got pregnant the first time. He was so proud when Jack was born. James Amos Robbins II was a fine specimen. The last name had been arbitrarily assigned directly after Stump's own birth. Willie Robbins was a well-respected member of the black community, and Papa borrowed his name without permission to stick it on his own illegitimate child.

"A baby a year followed for Stump and Macy until after your father's birth. Macy had a terrible time with his delivery and needed a hysterectomy a short time afterward. The surgery itself was rare for anyone back then, and especially among blacks, but Mama made arrangements with the doctor and paid for it out of her household money without Papa's knowledge when Stump told her how sick his wife was. The procedure was performed in the doctor's home. It's a wonder Macy didn't die. I think because she had such a tough time and because he was her last possible child, she spoiled your daddy more than she did the others. Probably without even realizing she did."

Miss Hattie rose from her position on the bed and walked to the window, staring out as she continued. "Stump and I continued to work side by side in the store with Till acting like the big boss. He didn't know one thing about business or dealing with the public, and without Stump we couldn't have made it. Papa's drinking was getting worse and worse and consumed all his waking hours. He died with a Mason jar of moonshine in his hand.

"Stump, Macy and their children sat with Mama and me at the funeral. It had not been discussed beforehand, and I just assumed that's the way it would be. After all the neighbors had left the house that night, I got my first beating at the hand of my husband. He had browbeaten me since the wedding, but he had never hit me before. I moved into the room next door to our bedroom, Stump's and Missy's old room, locked the door each night, and would not let him touch me.

"Not until the night fifteen years later when in a drunken rage he raped me. Zell was the result of that awful experience, and perhaps I never forgave my son for that. I know he was not to blame and knew it then, but he was evil like his father from the beginning. I tried so hard to make him gentle like Mama and Stump, but Till worked just as hard to create the monster you saw. After a while, I gave up. I loved him as my child but hated his wicked spirit. Thankfully Mama died before he was a year old, and she never saw how truly mean he was.

"She had been such a good mother to Missy, Stump, and me that I wanted to be just like her. Till and Zell wouldn't allow me. The fact that I was so old when he was born probably also contributed to the lack of intimacy between my only offspring and me. Whatever the cause, it broke my heart. And my spirit."

She turned back to face Jane, tears streaming down her cheeks, and once more took her spot beside the younger woman on the bed. She continued. "During all this, Till and I naturally grew farther and farther apart, and Stump and I remained the close siblings we had always been. I kept abreast of Macy and the children through the letters Lynn told you about and during my workdays with Stump. I was not allowed to visit in their home, of course, nor they in mine. Till really would have killed me. Stump's wife and children really weren't even welcome in the store.

"Till was developing a real hatred for Stump, whose intelligence and comfort with the customers served to accentuate Till's lack of both. I should have recognized the danger I was putting Stump in and insisted that he find a job somewhere else, but I so selfishly wanted to keep him near me for my protection and for companionship. I chose to ignore Till's derogatory remarks and crude comments in an effort to keep my beloved brother at my side."

Once again, the narrator arose and walked to the dresser where she retrieved a box of tissues. She wiped her eyes and nose with one and took the box back with her to the bed where she resumed her spot and the story. "The day Till fired the fatal shot, Stump had just taken a tongue lashing in front of a group of customers but, as always, had not opened his mouth in return. Till chastised him for leaving a large slab of bacon out of the cooler overnight on the meat counter, rendering it unfit. Stump wrapped it in butcher paper and carried it outside to the latest in a long line of worthless curs till kept behind the store. I knew, and both of them knew, that it was Till who had taken the meat out the night before to cut some for that same dog before we closed for the day. It was just another chance to denigrate the 'nigger' in front of the locals. It didn't work then as it had never worked before, and that made Till even madder. After the last customer had left, he then turned his wrath on me.

"I was in the back room getting cloths and disinfectant to clean the meat counter when he slipped in unnoticed behind me, closed the door, and started choking me without so much as a word. I couldn't utter a sound, but I dropped the galvanized metal bucket I had been holding, and Stump heard the crash. He came running and pulled the beast off me. He was helping me to compose myself and clean up the mess

I had dropped when Till crept in behind and shot him point blank; I thought my life was over. Everything good I had ever known was dead."

She stopped and stared for a moment at Jane whose tears were now flowing. With no more of her own to wipe, Miss Hattie reached and cleared those from Jane's cheeks before continuing. "I merely went through the motions of living after that and withdrew from the world except for Macy and her family. The communication methods left much to be desired, but I meant never to lose contact. Years later when Zell convinced Lynn to marry him, I should have tried to stop the plans for her sake, but I was so starved for real human companionship, I didn't. I even encouraged it. For me, it was a blessing; for her it was the worst of nightmares. Through guilt and love, I tried to soften the blow, both figuratively and literally, when possible, but it wasn't often possible."

Jane wiped her eyes, blew her nose, and again inquired as to who was privy to all this information. "And Uncle Jack knows all this?"

"He knows the facts. He doesn't know my feelings and angles on things; although I'm sure he figured out how I felt. It was my decision not to tell you, and everyone has graciously honored that decision. I wanted to wait until I felt you were ready. I saw how bitter you were at such an early age, and I wasn't sure you could deal with the fact that Zell was your cousin."

As if that fact had not previously sunk in, Jane shivered and blinked before responding. "You're right. I'm not sure I could have either. Sorry, but it's much easier with him dead. I just hate that you had to bear this burden so long alone."

"Oh, I wasn't alone," Miss Hattie quickly countered. "Your family (actually my family, too) always were there, lending an emotional as well as physical hand. We were fortunate that both Jack and Pie married such good women who could handle this rather unlikely group. Can't say much for your

Uncle Bud, though. We never did figure how he got into the group."

For the first time since the opening revelation, both women seemed to find real humor in the last statement and doubled over in convulsive laughter, made more emotional by their desperate need for some sort of release. Lynn came into the room at that moment, a quizzical look on her face. "I've lain awake nights trying to play out how this moment would actually go, but I certainly never expected it to be a laughing matter for either of you. Are y'all all right?"

Jane was the first to suppress her giggles. "There is not much to laugh about in any of this, for sure, but poor old dead Uncle Bud's name came up, and we couldn't resist the urge."

With that, the two new confidants again burst into squeals. Lynn excused herself with the same confused look she had worn into the room and returned to the kitchen, once again leaving them alone.

When the giggling had worn itself out, Miss Hattie spoke very seriously. "I have so many things I'm ashamed of. I could have made Missy's life easier. I could have insisted they untie Stump's hand instead of sneaking around and untying it when no one was looking. I could have announced to the world that Stump was my adored brother; standards be damned! I could have refused that monster's marriage proposal. Perhaps I could have prevented Lynn from ruining her life. I could have loved Zell more, and then maybe none of the last tragedy would have happened. I'll never know the answer to that, but I'll spend what little time I have left wondering."

"Miss Hattie," Jane snapped, "for the first time today, what you are saying is not making sense. In fact, it's utter nonsense! You had no choice in most of the issues you're worrying about. Okay, so maybe you could have prevented the marriages, but who knows what difference that would have made. Lynn was pretty much without options when she and

Zell married, or so the opinions of that time dictated. And while I'm not sure anything positive came from yours and Mr. Till's marriage, it seems to me you're the only one who suffered from it."

"How can you possibly be so kind, Jane Ellen?" an incredulous lady demanded. "The thing I feel most ashamed of is Stump's death. Had I not married that thing, he would have been spared."

"Circumstances beyond our control rule our lives so much of the time. Those were just such circumstances. Mr. Till was responsible for Papa's death. Nobody else. If you have any doubts as to my lack of ill will or anger toward you, let me put them to rest for you. I have nothing but respect and admiration for you and what you have felt and done for the people I love and have loved." Jane attempted to assure her.

With that the old lady burst into tears and grabbed Jane in a warm embrace. "I've waited so long to hear that from you. I know I don't have long to live. Couldn't. I'm nearly ninety years old, for goodness sake, and I want to make my peace with everybody whose lives I have adversely affected, if at all possible. You and Lynn are the last ones. Lynn assures me she has nothing to forgive, but I know better. She has been so good to me. A daughter couldn't have cared for me more, and I have been so richly blessed by being able to transfer some of the love I wanted to give my natural child to her.

"I have one more thing I need to show you. I have wanted to since Zell's funeral, but Lynn wouldn't let me. She wanted the timing to be right. We had to make sure the grand jury issue was settled first."

She walked back to the trunk from which she had taken the photo album; this time she brought out what looked to be a miniature cedar chest from which she retrieved a letter, handing it unopened to Jane. "Read this; I received it the week before Zell's death."

Jane tentatively opened the one-page typewritten missive, feeling as if she were invading the privacy of her hostess. She scanned the correspondence, missing its significance. It was an offer from a Montgomery attorney to lease Miss Hattie's twelve-hundred-acre estate for twenty-five years and what Jane thought an ungodly high rate.

"I'm afraid I don't understand what this letter has to do with me, Miss Hattie."

Again Lynn appeared, but this time she settled herself with them on the bed and explained. "When Miss Hattie got this, it was addressed to her alone. She shared its content with me before discussing it with Zell because she was so torn as to what to do. The store was losing money daily, and we would have already starved if not for Jack and Pie. She knew Zell's reaction would be to grab the money and live a life of luxury for as long as it held out, but again she felt guilty."

"It wasn't mine nor Zell's to control, I didn't think," Miss Hattie piped in. "Although Papa had left it exclusively to me, I always knew it was just as much Stump's family's as mine. I finally got the courage to show the letter to Zell and to tell him how it had to be settled. I never saw him lose control quite so completely.

"He had stayed at the store extremely late, drinking as usual. We had nowhere to go, nobody to go to, but Lynn and I left and drove around aimlessly for a while, hoping he would cool off. This was not the first time we had to leave like that. We were gone about an hour."

It was again Lynn's turn to speak. "By the time we got back home, he had continued drinking as much as he could consume, but not before he ransacked the house looking for the letter Miss Hattie had had the presence of mind to grab as we made our hasty retreat.

"We thought he was out cold when we returned and found him lying across his bed. We were trying to reestablish some order in here when he roused and came in on us. He was further incensed that we were working together. He always accused us of conspiring against him. He came toward me with a pistol I didn't even know he owned. I knelt on the floor, prepared to die."

"Thankfully he was in worse shape than he thought, though." contributed Miss Hattie, "and he tripped over the edge of the rug. I wrestled the gun from him while Lynn cowered on the floor. That's when he turned on me. I ran, gun in hand, to the front of the house and screamed for Lynn to leave out the back. She refused, of course, concerned for my safety, and followed us into the living room, where he continued to come toward me, with Lynn yelling to him and begging him to sleep it off and not hurt anyone.

"He was calling me all kinds of names, the least of which you saw on the mirror that night. He even spat on me, told me he hated me, always had, because my brother was black. He started toward me to hit me, something he had never done before. I snapped.

"I finally had within my power the means to do something positive. I could stop the suffering I had caused or whose cause I had overlooked all those years. I shot him with my one goal being his death, and of all my actions, that is the one I am not ashamed of."

What were these people telling her? That Miss Hattie, not Lynn, killed Zell? That it was perhaps not self defense, after all, but murder, mother of son? Of course! The room she had believed to be Lynn's was Miss Hattie's. She had moved with ease within it this morning. The message on the mirror that night had been for his mother, the sister of a black, rather than for his wife.

Lynn's strange behavior before the grand jury's convening, the fact that Miss Hattie still loved her daughter-in-law as she did following Zell's death, and Miss Hattie's isolation all made sense now. It had never been Miss Hattie trying to protect Lynn; it was Lynn who had been trying to protect Miss Hattie. What was Jane to do with this revelation? She was the sheriff.

Lynn broke into Jan's reverie. "I tried to convince Miss Hattie never to tell any of this to anyone. No one but the two of us ever had to know, but she insisted you did. I hope your compassion can extend farther that your professionalism and you can see this for what it is—self-defense born of years of personal and societal abuse. Can you do that and pretend this conversation never took place? Miss Hattie has nobody but us, her family, to make sure the time she has left is as happy as possible. Surely you can see she deserves that?"

Miss Hattie spoke resolutely. "I tried to tell the truth that awful night, but Lynn wouldn't hear of it. Everybody knew what a horrible existence hers had been as Zell's wife, and she convinced me that she could handle the public pressure better than I could.

"Nobody ever really asked either of us what happened; so it wasn't as if we actually lied. We just let you all think what you chose to think. Lynn was in terrible shape from a beating he had given her earlier that evening, before he got so drunk. We were afraid someone would notice that some of the places were already bruising, but nobody said anything.

"Then when you offered to get her into bed, we both panicked. But again you assumed the room with all the damage was hers, and we didn't tell you otherwise. We didn't think to wipe my prints off the gun and let Lynn hold it, but so many people handled it after the investigators arrived, again because everyone assumed Lynn had used it, we felt confidant it wouldn't be checked.

"One thing we both agreed on was that I not go out of the house at all until after the grand jury met. That way I couldn't slip and give any information that would reveal the true course of events. I can assure you I would never have allowed Lynn to go to jail. She argued with me even on that point, but that's where I drew the line.

"I'm sorry we were less than honest with you, but we both knew how truly professional you were, and Lynn worried that you couldn't respect our wishes. If you can't see fit to leave this as it is, that's okay with me. There are some loose ends I must tie up before I die, and your knowing the true story was one of them."

This was too much to try to assimilate. A great portion of what Jane had believed to be had just been revealed as false, and things she had always viewed as black and white now faded into a large gray area.

Miss Hattie once again interrupted her thinking. "There's one more thing I want to discuss with you, but only after you've had a chance to sleep on all this. Promise me one thing though; you mustn't tell a soul one word we've discussed here until we've talked again. Lynn and I will be going to church tomorrow, and I'm sure you will, too. Meet us back here tomorrow afternoon at one for a light lunch and further discussion. Can I count on you for that?"

Jane released a pent-up sigh and promised, "Of course you can. There are so many things I need to try to get straight within my own mind, but I can assure you, I'll tell no one."

Lynn walked her to the door while Miss Hattie replaced the objects that had caused the stir. When they got to the kitchen, Lynn pleaded her case. "Jane, you must understand that she is a very old lady. She has had such a difficult time most of her life, and she truly feels she has done the world a good deed by killing her own son. I'm not sure there is a person who knew him who could honestly argue otherwise. But the whole ordeal has been a nightmare for her. Nothing can be gained by revealing what really happened to Zell.

"He died because he was being abusive and threatening. What difference can it possibly make now that it was at her hand rather than mine? You know as well as I do that she would get the same reaction from a grand jury as I did. I just knew I could handle it better than she could. I honestly believe it would have killed her, and I'm not sure I could have dealt with that. Besides, I didn't care, still don't, one bit about what the community thinks.

"Please, leave it alone, for her sake. You know I'm not a dishonest person. I just don't see how pursuing this could benefit anyone."

Jane hugged her friend and promised to consider it seriously but gave no indication what her decision would be. She couldn't; she had no idea herself.

Chapter XX

The remainder of that day and the long night that followed were spent in the greatest introspection of her life. She pored over Papa's Bible and considered its history, a history she had just learned, as she once again heard in her mind's ear Papa's deep voice entertaining her with stories he had learned at his white mother's knee. She sniffed again the limp yellowing paper within the book's pages and imagined herself that young impressionable girl again. She even pulled one of the expensive dolls from its storage shelf and remembered anew the pleasure she had acquired from those whose lives had touched hers but who were now gone. How would they have reacted to her current dilemma?

With the facts of Papa's origin so fresh in her own mind, it was particularly his mind she would have chosen to pick. This was his beloved sister whose whole life lay in her hands. A sister he had loved enough to risk his life for daily and to give that life for her ultimately. Even though Jane had been so young when he died, it was he who had taught her the value of family and the importance of sticking together at all times and at all costs.

But Jane was sworn to uphold the law for all the citizens, not just to preserve her family tree. Papa had also taught her love of order and obedience to the law. Would she have been confused if this recent information had been revealed about some other family in the county?

This inner struggle and all its attendant questions kept her awake most of the night. In fact, it was almost daylight before she slept at all, and then only fitfully. She awoke for church far from rested. However, she knew she needed divine guidance as she never had before; so she pulled herself from bed, dressed, and made the drive to the same country church she had worshipped in as a child,; back then with her grandparents.

It was a beautiful day, and the entire world seemed awash with the blooms that were the South in the spring and summer. She slipped quietly into her usual pew but participated only half heartedly in the preliminaries. Neither the words of the hymns nor the prayers of the minister got past her own musings. It was not until Reverend Deason announced the text for his sermon that she really heard anything outside her own head. The scripture was from Daniel . She had her answer. Papa was speaking to her as clearly as he had in that straight-back chair when he first laughed at her for her mispronunciations of the principal characters in this the story of Daniel's dilemma in the lion's den.

There comes a time when the laws of man must be circumvented to protect greater things. In Shadrach, Meshach, and Abednego's case, it had been the preservation of God's superiority that was the greater thing. In her case, it was the preservation of an old woman's life—a life that had had little value before. And she also knew at that moment that regardless of whose family it had been, she would have felt the same.

She thanked God and Papa for the wisdom and hurried out of church during the last hymn, before the benediction, to deliver her decision to Miss Hattie and Lynn.

It was only 12:30 when she wheeled into the driveway, and she didn't wait for an invitation before bursting through the screen door of the kitchen. Instead, she raced into the room, causing the two startled ladies inside to put down the pimento and cheese they were spreading on bread to stare at her.

"You were right," she practically screamed. "Papa told me. I have never felt so sure about anything in my life. The hatred and fear can finally come to an end. I will never tell anyone what you told me yesterday. Now can we eat? I'm starved. I haven't had a bite since our last meal together."

The hugging and crying continued for quite some time, but the laughter that followed around the table was more than either of the three of them had allowed themselves in ages. Again, conversation was inconsequential and light until every crumb had been consumed and the dishes stacked into the sink. Then Miss Hattie presented Jane with the last detail she had promised from the day before.

"Jane Ellen, I showed you the letter from the attorney concerning rental of the land. Since none of the family has any interest in farming now and since it has been virtually useless for the last twenty or so years, I would like to suggest that I sign the agreement. It seems a generous offer to me. What do you think?"

"Miss Hattie, it seems like a very good deal to me, too, but I don't know why my opinion counts; I'm certainly not an expert in such matters," a bewildered Jane replied.

"The reason I want your opinion is because all this directly affects you," Miss Hattie began her explanation. "You are my brother's granddaughter, and this land belongs to all my family. I intend to share our decision with the remainder of our relatives, but I had to clear up the matter of Zell's death before I proceeded with this.

"I entreat you to agree to be the executor of my estate at the time of my death. If you can get away from your office sometime next week, I would like for the two of us to drive to Montgomery for a meeting with my lawyer. With your permission, I want to rewrite my will and establish the ground rules for the property rental.

"The proceeds from the lease are to be divided equally among all my family, and that includes Lynn, of course. Following my death, all my belongings, and there are few other than the land, are to be dispersed among all of you. The only thing I'm waiting for is your decision. What do you say?"

"I say I'm dumbfounded. You've certainly given me plenty to think about the last two days. I'm flattered that you honor me so, but I don't feel worthy. First of all, you don't owe me or any other member of my part of the family anything. Secondly, there are others much more qualified than I to handle your affairs."

"I want it understood up front that I'm not doing this because I feel I owe anybody anything. I'm doing it out of love and a desire to make things right...finally. Please, humor me; let me do this. As to there being others more qualified, I've watched you since you returned and kept up with you while you were away and believe you know what you're doing. And I can't think of anybody else I would trust more to do what's fair to everybody concerned. Please tell me you'll do it," Miss Hattie pleaded.

"What about Lynn?" Jane asked. "Why can't she handle your affairs? She knows about your personal business."

"She does, and we've discussed it, but she agrees with me that your training and background make you the more logical choice. She has no experience in the business world. This is not an insult to her and the love she has shown me. I would not have asked you without her blessings," Miss Hattie assured her.

"Absolutely!" Lynn piped in. "I would be lost even trying to attend to it. I will help both of you in any way I can, but you must say you'll be primarily responsible, Jane."

"All right, I'll do it," Jane agreed. "But I do think you're being away too generous. You need to reserve a large portion of the rental income for yourself. It can be divided according to your instructions at your death."

"Absolutely not!" Miss Hattie emphasized. "I have spent so many years surrounded by unhappiness and emotional deprivation. I want to see some joy in my last days. I hope this windfall will bring your family some contentment and freedom from financial worries and that they will allow me the pleasure of knowing I contributed in some small way."

"You and I both know Uncle Jack's family will be ecstatic. He works so hard and barely gets by. Who knows about Aunt Sami's crowd. Are you sure you want to give them free reign with any money. You know how they are," Jane reasoned.

"I do, and they will probably squander part, if not all, of it, but we can only pray they will put some of it to good use. They're Stump's family, too, and he would have done the same," Miss Hattie assured her.

"You seem to be intent on doing this, and I want to do what you want," Jane relented. "I'll be happy to drive you to your lawyer's office to make the arrangements. I'll call Donny later this afternoon and have him cover for me tomorrow morning. We can go then."

A teary-eyed Miss Hattie rose from her chair and grabbed an unsuspecting Jane in a bear hug. "You have made me a very happy old woman!" she exclaimed. "Now we must tell the others. Get them on the phone for me, please, Lynn."

"Miss Hattie, if you don't mind let's wait. I'd like to have you all over Friday night for dinner. It just seems appropriate that an announcement of this magnitude be made over a family meal. Around the kitchen table is where we held all our family discussions when I was young. Papa and Mama would like it that way, I think," Jane offered.

"You're absolutely right, Jane Ellen," Miss Hattie offered. "That would be a delightful treat for me to share a meal with all of you."

So it was that on a star-studded Friday night in a small antebellum cottage in a tiny Southern town, four generations of a family previously divided by race, social station, hatred, and ignorance united for the first time around a table laden with traditional cooking.

They laughed, they cried, they embraced, they exchanged stories, and they rejoiced in their newly discovered relationships. And Jane wondered if she was the only one who felt the comforting presence of several additional unseen, yet most delighted, guests.